Praise for JoAnn Smith Ainsworth's *Out of the Dark*

"Out of the Dark is an absolutely fantastic book. ...this is the best historical romance I have read in months. Superb presentation of the characters ...Thanks to Ms Ainsworth, Out of the Dark is a definite keeper and one I completely recommend."

~ *Anya, Coffee Time Romance*

"I enjoyed Out of the Dark. I especially found the relationship between the tough mother and the intellectual father intriguing....Check your stock characters at the door. The two have a solid (yet different) relationship with mutual respect for each other."

~ *Enduring Romance*

"'Heartwarming medieval tale!' MATILDA'S SONG is a story of love, loyalty and betrayal. JoAnn Smith Ainsworth has written a very realistic story of life back in the days after the Normans defeated the Saxons in medieval England. ...If you enjoy a good medieval tale, don't miss this one."

~ *Chere Gruver, ParaNormalRomance.org*

"Out of the Dark is an interesting book. Lynnet is not made out to be a weakling despite her blindness..."

~ *Tori, Joyfully Reviewed*

"...This story really shows the class struggle and the hardships people had to overcome to love outside of their social status. The story is very well written. You will laugh, cry, hold your breath, and cheer with these characters. I found myself pulled right into this story from the first page, and was sad when I realized I had read the last word. Matilda's Song is one of the best books I have read this year."

~ *LeeAnn, Coffee Time Romance*

Look for these titles by
JoAnn Smith Ainsworth

Now Available:

Matilda's Song

Out of the Dark

JoAnn Smith Ainsworth

A Samhain Publishing, Ltd. publication.

Samhain Publishing, Ltd.
577 Mulberry Street, Suite 1520
Macon, GA 31201
www.samhainpublishing.com

Out of the Dark

Print ISBN: 978-1-60504-277-0
Digital ISBN: 1-59998-941-7

Editing by Bethany Morgan
Cover by Anne Cain

First Samhain Publishing, Ltd. electronic publication: May 2008
First Samhain Publishing, Ltd. print publication: March 2009

Dedication

To my son, Dennis.

Thanks to my friend, Virginia McQuiston Peach, who read the first draft aloud to me, to the many friends who read early drafts and gave me encouragement, and to the members of the Willits Creative Writing Class—especially Evelyn Swift and its teacher, Carole Dawson, for their line edits.

Special thanks to my fabulous critique partners—Kathy Farrell and Desirae L. King—and to Lynne Laird, retired instructor, California School for the Blind.

Chapter One

November 1120 A.D., Britain

Royal Residence, Tower of London

"If evil took up residence in walls," Lady Lynnet muttered to herself, "these cellars would be the perfect place for it."

She wrinkled her nose as she ran sensitive fingertips along the corridor's massive stones. Forty years of royal habitation left behind vile smells.

Stone corridors pressed threateningly in on her despite being wide enough to allow armored knights to pass with ease. They reminded her that this Norman castle, bordering on the befouled River Thames, was built inside a fortress housing its own armories and garrisoned soldiers.

Lynnet was having difficulty finding her way back to the chambers assigned to her by King Henry. The dim, grayed shadows that were her constant companions since illness took most of her sight at eight years old failed to provide shapes to guide her. In these lower passageways, torches were few and far between, making variations of light and dark nearly nonexistent and disorienting to her.

"I'm lost."

The realization made the small hairs at the back of her neck stand on end.

"Anyone here?" she shouted, her voice cracking from distress.

The thickness of the walls absorbed the sound. No footsteps echoed through the corridors, no voices of soldiers returning from guard duty or servants hauling foodstuffs to storerooms. The unusual silence was worrisome.

"God's truth, they must be in the Great Hall for midday meal."

No one would be worried and looking for her. Evelyn, her companion and personal servant, thought she was with her parents. Her parents thought she'd returned to her own chamber after their argument about her suitors—or lack thereof. It could be hours before these subterranean passageways again filled with people returning from their meal. Hours she'd be alone, in the silence, in the dark. With the rats. She shivered.

"I'll find my own way."

Her fingers searched beneath the supple wool draping her neckline and froze when they encountered nothing.

"My good luck charm! It's gone!"

Bequeathed to her by her paternal grandmother, the crystal pendant quickly had become her talisman against evil. While wearing it, the guiding spirit of her beloved grandmamma seemed near, keeping her from harm. She felt inside her clothing, hoping the necklace lodged there. Nothing.

Lynnet tried to swallow, but her dry mouth wouldn't cooperate. Fear rose. Inborn stubbornness, daily driving her towards independence, melted away. Without her protective talisman, she was exposed, vulnerable.

Realizing she was spiraling into a frenzied state, Lynnet reprimanded herself and restrained her mounting anxiety. Until being forced to accept defeat, she'd do her determined best to find her own way.

"Before I lost my sight, I played in these corridors. I don't need my crystal."

Lynnet tried to remember how far she'd traveled along the passageways, just how many turns she'd taken down the winding stairwell before becoming stranded on the wrong floor. Angry at her parents, she'd distractedly rushed along, foolishly not counting doorways or steps. Realization that she was lost dawned on her only after chilled cellar air forced her to tighten her woolen cloak around her shoulders.

Spots of brightness from burning torches, evenly spaced along the left corridor wall, emerged out of the surrounding gloom. The lighted torches were well above her head so she could not take one with her. She was shorter and more slender than most women, a disadvantage in a section of the castle meant for towering knights and their servants.

"If nothing else, I'll sit under a torch until a servant comes to replace it," she said with a wry smile.

Trailing fingers along the rough-edged stone wall, she walked cautiously, her mind searching outwards, trying to recognize where she was.

When she located an open doorway, she sniffed and allowed the atmosphere of the room to come to her. She definitely smelled potatoes.

"The last thing I need is to get trapped in some storeroom."

Lynnet stepped warily across the wide-open space, one foot in front of the other, until her right hand touched the opposite frame of the doorway. She continued to work her way along the passageway, disappointment plaguing her when she found no stairwells. Coming upon two closed doors, she took the time to open them and listen to make sure no one was working in there.

At a cross corridor, out of long-standing habit, she turned in her favorite direction—right. After a few steps, she stopped to listen. In the distance, she heard muffled voices.

"God's mercy."

Relief passed through her, making her aware her knees had been trembling. She had not realized how fearful she'd become until her anxiety fled.

Lynnet hurried towards the voices, remembering to trail her fingertips along the chiseled corridor wall. When close enough to distinguish the words spoken, she reined herself abruptly to a standstill. The shiver that traveled along her spine had nothing to do with the cellar's cold air.

"Destroy the vile Saxon hellspawn," said a man with a slight northern accent. "Crush them once and for all."

"...chaos...kingdom..." a second man said in a whiny, nasal voice.

"...king's brother...malleable...murder."

The cultured voice of the third man belied the evil in the words spoken.

Alarmed, Lynnet turned around and headed back the way she had come. Her heart pounded loudly in her ears and pressure built in her forehead.

Near these Normans is no place for an Anglo-Saxon.

Her soft-soled slippers barely made a sound as she sped along the now familiar corridor. Its coarse stone assaulted her fingertips. She rounded the corner, praying she'd done nothing to bring herself to the notice of these evildoers who spoke secretively of murder and chaos.

Scraping sounds warned Lynnet that men wearing armor were rising to their feet.

They could be soldiers or even knights. For certain, they're not the kitchen help.

Lynnet crossed to the dark side of the corridor so torchlight wouldn't reflect off her flaxen hair.

I'm grateful Evelyn dressed me in dark colors today.

Muffled voices bid each other farewell. Was she far enough away they couldn't see her? She pulled her cloak up over her light-colored hair to shroud her pale face and hide her exposed hands. Panicked, she forced herself to walk faster. She hoped the corridor was nearly as dark to them as it appeared to her.

She hurried past the two closed doors, worrying that the upcoming, open doorway might slow her down.

How much farther to the stairs?

Approaching footsteps confirmed at least two of the men were striding down her corridor.

Breathing in ragged gasps, Lynnet risked all. She ran towards a black spot she hoped was the open door, the opening now a haven instead of an obstacle.

"What's that?"

"Where?"

"Near the end of the hall."

Gall rose in Lynnet's throat, leaving a bitter taste. She touched the doorframe and entered the musty storeroom. Exploring with her hands, Lynnet struggled to find a hiding place. She choked back a shriek when a furry animal brushed by her outstretched hand and scurried away.

"You saw that cat."

"What I saw was too big for a cat."

The whiny voice sounded peeved.

"I think you're fencing at shadows," the cultured voice said. "Get a grip on yourself."

Stumbling, Lynnet knocked over what smelled like a basket of potatoes.

"Fencing at shadows, am I?"

The men started running towards the storeroom.

Lynnet's hand touched an empty crate. She crouched down, lifted the wooden crate and quietly dropped it over herself. Feeling around, she made certain its rim was solid to the floor and no piece of clothing escaped to reveal her hiding place. Boots pounded on the cellar pavement and armor jangled as the men approached.

"Shine your torch in here." The voice belonged to the man who had talked about murder.

Torchlight seeped between crate slats, but not enough to outline the men who hunted her.

"No one's here."

"He has to be. No one fled down the corridor."

"Perhaps there's a trap door."

Lynnet heard footsteps coming from the opposite direction in the corridor.

Oh, no. Not more of them.

"What's that?" the petulant voice hissed.

"Someone's coming. We can't be seen together. Put out that torch."

Lynnet listened to the two men hurry out the door. As their footsteps receded, the latest heavy footsteps came inevitably closer.

Torchlight again probed her hiding place. The pounding increased in her ears as she heard an angry, bass voice say, "Hell's bells."

ꕥ

His blood boiled. Supplies stored under the very feet of the king were disappearing and he, Basil of Ipswich, Sheriff of London, may have just missed the culprits.

He'd heard voices as he descended the wide, stone steps to the cellars, but thought nothing of it since castle servants and soldiers traversed these dark hallways. It was only when the light from his torch revealed the jumbled pile of potatoes that he realized the voices he heard could have been the pilferers. He stepped back outside the storeroom to look both ways. There was no sign of them in the torch-lit hallway.

"Blackhearted curs."

Basil had ridden to the Tower to assess the magnitude of the investigation laid upon his shoulders that morning by King Henry. He needed to know just what was stored in these cellars, how much had gone missing and how it was secured.

Unlocked storerooms better be the exception and not the rule.

A tedious inventory could've been avoided if he'd caught the miscreants. He much preferred dragging thieves off to jail to counting baskets of potatoes. Still, winter food supplies were important to the Crown. He'd do his best to see that no more went missing.

The sheriff stepped back inside and looked around. He knew this neglected clutter was not caused by a retainer or a soldier. A castle servant would have re-packed the potatoes or risked his livelihood. A soldier would have summoned a servant to clear it, just as Basil would soon do. The upturned crate and spilled potatoes bespoke a hasty retreat. The thieves were unable to take the pilfered booty with them.

The dishonor to the crown enraged Basil.

The monks who educated him taught him to act honorably and to be of service to others. King Henry's policies made life easier for citizens than those of the last king. To steal was unconscionable. To steal from this openhearted king deserved death. It was within Basil's power to see justice done. He would not shirk his duty.

He stuck his rush light into a wall sconce and took a quick look around the large storeroom. Its thick walls were lined with stacked wooden cartons and bulging bags of flours.

Basil reached down to upright a crate.

"What?"

A woman. Hidden under the storage crate!

She was a tiny thing, slender, with huge blue eyes in an oval face. His body responded to her beauty.

Strands of silken hair escaped a loosely woven, black netting to stick out awkwardly around her face. Bits of packing straw and dirt clung to the netting and to her dark clothing. Her lips hardened into a grim line.

She can't be one of the thieves, can she?

Outraged that he allowed her beauty to distract him from the king's business, he grasped her arm above the elbow, surprised at how fine-boned it was.

I could easily snap it in two.

He shook her to loosen her tongue.

"Why are you hiding?"

As she rose to her feet, he could see that her attire was that of a lady. Basil eased up on the pressure.

"Answer me."

She struggled, causing him little discomfort, even after kicking his shin with her soft-leather slipper.

"Unprincipled ruffian. My parents have influence with the king. They'll have your head if you harm me."

Basil pointed to the Seal of Office on a wide, blue ribbon around his neck.

"I'm the king's sheriff. I uphold the law, not break it." He gestured towards the spilled potatoes. "Are you stealing these?"

Twisting her arm out of his grasp, she drew herself up to her full height, barely reaching his armpit.

"Lackwitted underling, I'm lost. I came too far down the stairs and ended up in the cellars instead of at the Great Hall."

As she took a deep breath, her dark wool kirtle stretched enticingly over a rounded bosom. Basil allowed his eyes to linger there as he interrogated her.

"The stairwell is only a short distance."

"I'm blind. I couldn't find it."

"Blind?"

His brain became a jumble. Those bewitching blue eyes couldn't see? He shook his head, trying to clear it and re-focus on his duty.

"Who were those men?"

"I don't know. That's why I hid."

A change passed briefly over her face as she denied knowing the men. It was impossible to tell if she was lying or if the change was caused by the flickering of the rush light.

"Were they stealing potatoes?"

She shook her head.

"They wore armor. They don't need to steal food."

So it wasn't thieves who left hurriedly. He hadn't let down his king.

"Why didn't you ask them for help?"

"I didn't trust them, and I don't trust you. They're Norman."

Her sharp tongue sent acid rushing into his stomach. Early on, his mother instilled pride in his Norman ancestry. She also taught Anglo-Saxon inferiority. Blind or not, this woman touched a sore spot. He stiffened his spine.

"I'm the king's sheriff."

"Sheriffs can be bought. Even the highest in the land cannot be trusted."

Anger surged through Basil. His fingers curled into a fist.

"Do you malign the king?"

"Not the king, but those around him."

Was this the typical whining of a conquered Saxon or did she bear a legitimate gripe? Whatever it was, he was in no mood to stand around arguing. His duty was to catch thieves.

Basil's inherent need to protect those weaker than himself rose to the surface.

"I'll take you to a safe place."

Lynnet dusted herself off and set her clothes aright to recapture her dignity while she decided whether to trust this man.

His towering, muscled body cast a huge, black outline against the feeble light of the torch. Power and domination emanated from this sheriff, and it frightened her. His was the northern accent of the third conspirator. They could know each other. Even be related.

Besides, he was the kind of man she should shy away from, the savage warrior she remembered from jousts before losing her sight. She should've put up more of a fight when he first uncovered her, but she'd quickly lost the heart for it.

"Give me your father's name and the chamber you occupy."

Shivers traveled up her spine from the timbre of his voice. Lynnet heard the words as if from afar. Her usually superb hearing filtered through a thickening fog. Her clever mind, which grasped new teachings with ease, acted befuddled.

The clang of metal weaponry made it easy for her to follow his movements. The aroma of leather and horse clung to him. He provoked unsettled sensations in her groin.

"I assume this belongs to you."

He had reached into his clothing and was placing a chain and pendant into her hand. Its metal was warm from his body.

"I found this on the stairs."

Her hand closed around the familiar crystal. She slipped the warmed chain around her neck and sighed as the pendant nestled between her breasts. She was again protected by Grandmamma's amulet.

"Woman, what chamber do you occupy?" He repeated his demand, sounding annoyed.

Sensations, however pleasant, must be denied or she might sacrifice her life for her curiosity. The earlier, overheard words placed her in jeopardy. The sheriff sounded like one of the three men.

I must get myself back to my family, and quickly.

She'd just have to trust him. For now.

"Wilfgive of Osfrith. The Rose Chamber."

Basil was fuming.

She's stubborn, closed mouth and fighting me at every turn. She's too independent for her own good. She acts as if we're at war and everything is a state secret.

He'd gotten her name, but only after convincing her that, since he knew her father's name, it would be easy enough to inquire and learn hers.

Basil's frustration mounted with this blind woman whose fingertips lightly touched his forearm as he guided her out of the cellars. He was convinced there was more to her hiding than she'd admitted. Perhaps her virtue had been threatened. He was resentful that her lack of candor required him to set aside the king's investigation to see to her safety. Many sheriffs would ignore the plight of a Saxon, but Basil was taught by monks. He'd see justice done.

Reaching the level for the Rose Chamber, he stepped out of the stairwell. Because she irritated him by her intransigence, he wasn't feeling particularly accommodating and deliberately, without warning, turned the corner abruptly into her corridor. He was astounded when she easily followed.

Still stupefied, he gradually became aware she was speaking.

"And so you see, my parents won't take kindly to my being lost. I can make it on my own from here."

"I never leave a lady alone and unprotected."

She looked annoyed.

"You'd save me a lot of trouble. They'll not be happy with me."

"Your father and mother deserve to know you're safe."

She clutched his arm.

"Take me to my chamber first. I'll visit them as soon as I get cleaned up."

She sounded panicked, but he wasn't budging. Although he no longer believed her a thief, he'd keep digging until he learned the mystery behind her hiding under a wooden crate. If parental anger would release her tongue, so be it.

Basil stopped at the door of the Rose Chamber and raised

his hand to knock.

"Answer me truthfully and I'll consider taking you to your chamber. What did those men do to you?"

She hunched her shoulders and gritted her teeth.

"Nothing."

The sheriff knocked loudly.

Her richly-dressed father answered the door and Basil saw he looked puzzled upon seeing his untidy daughter.

"My dear, what happened?"

Lynnet was wringing her hands.

"I got lost in the cellars."

And more than that, if only she'd say.

"I am Basil of Ipswich, Sheriff of London. I found your daughter..."

"There's no problem, Father, although I must look a fright."

She presented her parents to him with formal introductions.

Her mother advanced on them, her face scornful. Lady Durwyn towered over both Lord Wilfgive and Lady Lynnet, her back upright and rigid as she chastised her daughter.

"You should know better than to wander off."

Other than the father's first words, Basil picked up no sense of caring directed towards the daughter.

No wonder she pleaded to clean up first.

"I'm concerned about your daughter. She was..."

"I was trying to find my way back," Lady Lynnet broke in. "I tripped over some potatoes and got scraped up. It's minor. Don't worry."

So that's how the potatoes got spilled.

"I've been trying to ask your daughter..."

Her mother shooed him out the door, her hands driving him away as if controlling a flock of chickens.

"Not now, Sheriff. I'll not have you questioning our daughter while she looks a disgrace."

He shook his head at the ill-mannered audacity of the woman.

Lady Durwyn pointed to the right, a rose-colored silk sleeve cascading downward from her outstretched arm.

"Knock next door and tell that servant to get over here fast if she knows what's good for her."

Basil watched, astounded, as the Rose Chamber door shut in his face.

"I'll play their lackey today," he grumbled as he approached the daughter's chamber door, "only because I must get back to the king's business. Eventually I'll find out what happened in the cellars."

"God's truth, I don't care what your parents said or did, you shouldn't have run off."

Evelyn, her companion, personal servant and friend since she lost her sight as a child, was upset with her.

"It's not like I thought about it. It just happened."

Lynnet was sitting on a stool. Her companion had arranged a basin of soapy water, a cloth and towel and her hairbrush on the table. She detected the faint hint of rosewater added to the water. A fresh set of clean clothing lay next to the basin. The pot of stew warming on the fireplace hook made her mouth water and her stomach growl with hunger.

Lynnet heard Evelyn dip the linen cloth into the basin of

water. She sat still, allowing her companion to wash the grime off her face and hands. Evelyn took advantage of their friendship to scold.

"Look at you. You're all dirty and your clothing is twisted about. You look more like a street waif than the lady you are."

"It was dirty down there."

She hadn't told anyone about her experiences in the cellars, only that she'd gotten lost. With the sheriff standing nearby, she'd held off telling her parents what she'd overheard even though it might affect the king.

The problem was she wasn't certain she'd heard correctly. The cellars distorted sounds. Then too, although the sheriff worked for the king, it was possible the three men were pledged to the crown as well. If they were corrupt, who was to say the sheriff was not corrupt.

The opportunity passed when her mother ordered the sheriff to summon Evelyn to get their daughter cleaned up and looking respectable.

Evelyn removed the netting with capable fingers and started brushing Lynnet's waist-length hair.

"What did your mother and father do this time to upset you?"

"The usual. Arguing—as if I'm not there—on the best way to marry me off and still keep our wealth intact."

Lynnet's mother was first cousin to the late queen. In Lady Durwyn's mind, the only hope for a suitable marriage was her daughter's superior breeding and family wealth. Even though her father's Wessex lands were appropriated by King William after the Battle of Hastings, the family still retained considerable wealth through her mother's Scottish estates. And she didn't let them forget it.

At seventeen, Lynnet was nearing spinsterhood. If her parents died while she was still unmarried, the king, as her guardian, might settle her in a nunnery and transfer her inheritance to a male relative. Or confiscate it for himself. Her parents wanted no excuse to transfer more lands into Norman hands.

“Once again, my mother was pointing out my inferiority as a marriage prospect because of my lack of vision.”

The mere thought of this old argument made her skin crawl.

Her companion clucked her tongue.

“They don’t know you like I do. Any man would be blessed to have you as his wife.”

At the time disease stole her sight, chickenpox claimed her older brother’s life and severely pock-marked her father. Her high-born parents never recovered. Embittered, they grieved that their only surviving child was female and flawed.

Illness cooled family relations with the crown. Normans were blamed for the tragedy since a foreign delegation brought the chickenpox. It was in the Tower that disease spread, devastating her family.

The scarring it caused was more than skin deep. After the Saxon Queen died, their visits devolved into a despised duty, tolerated only because the family could not be seen as snubbing a Norman king. Her mother’s cherished desire was to live on her own lands where Saxon superiority was well established and no one dared slight her.

Evelyn finished the brushing and was braiding her hair.

“As soon as my parents can get away from this duty of attending court, they’ll return home and find me a suitable husband of pure Anglo-Saxon descent.”

Lynnet wanted none of this. If she had to live with diminished sight, she at least deserved a man she cared for in her marriage bed. Not one only interested in wealth and social standing.

"What are my chances of finding a man to love at winter court?" she asked Evelyn. "Someone acceptable to my parents?"

"Naught."

The conspirators spoke quietly in a dark corner while guests mingled in the Great Hall, awaiting the king's arrival and the announcement to be seated for the evening meal.

"I overheard the father say that his daughter became lost in the cellars today."

The whiny voice of Count Maximilian de Selsey sounded anxious.

"So you were right," Sir André de Chester said, the flickering torch light reflecting from his thick, blond hair and emphasizing his hooked nose. "Someone was in the storeroom. It wasn't just the cat as Courbet insisted."

"I wonder where she was hiding? The Sheriff of London found her, blast his miserable, interfering hide."

André smirked.

"My half-brother has a habit of sticking his nose in where it doesn't belong."

André scratched his goateed chin as he looked around. The king's favorite hounds slept under the oak table where golden goblets marked the places for the king and his daughter. Hundreds of candles and torches lit walls hung with gigantic tapestries to dampen the cold. Fresh straw and evergreen needles covered the wide pavement stones on the floor, masking the stench from yesterday's rotting food droppings and animal feces. Minstrels played lyres and pipes from a mezzanine balcony.

"Which one is she?"

André flexed his muscles threateningly, making Maximilian anxious. His co-conspirator had a handsome face, but a black heart.

Maximilian gestured towards the opposite wall of the high vaulted Grand Hall. André had the height and breadth to make him feel inferior and Maximilian resented him for it.

"The one sitting on that bench in the shadows. She's blind. It doesn't matter that she sits where there's no light."

André smiled.

"Blind? Christ Jesus, that is providential for us. Has she spoken? Do we know if she overheard?"

"Not even a whisper. My Anglo-Saxon sister-in-law is a friend of the woman. I visited and heard no gossip."

"Good. No one must learn of our plans."

"She may not have heard a thing. The storeroom is far from our meeting place."

"A pox on this king," André said. "We made it look as if rebel Saxons are robbing his tax collectors and stealing his grain. His father would've taken an army out to slaughter them by now."

André's face darkened in anger. "To rid this land of the Anglo-Saxons, we may have to forcibly free his weak-kneed brother from Henry's imprisonment."

"We can bring him home from France to take over the kingdom."

Sir André straightened and stared across the Great Hall at Lady Lynnet.

"We'll have to make sure she doesn't talk."

Maximilian's stomach clenched. "No killings," he hissed. "Not in the king's residence. We're in deep enough as it is."

ꙮ

Lynnet had been uncertain all afternoon whether to involve her parents in what she overheard. She struggled with it all through evening meal. Now, they were back in their Tower chambers and she was decided.

"Father, Mother, I have to tell you what happened this morning."

As her mother turned against the candlelight, Lynnet saw by her outline that she still wore a tall, silken coif to cover her graying hair. Her parents believed in making a show of their wealth whenever they appeared in public.

"We know what happened," her mother said, sounding exasperated. "You got yourself lost just like we predicted." Her mother heaved a long sigh. "It's about time you learn to accept your limitations."

Lynnet dug her heels in. She lay a hand on her crystal pendant, rubbing it between thumb and forefinger to sustain her courage.

"I overheard some men talking. I think they're plotting against the king."

"Another flight of fancy, Daughter?" Her mother's tongue sounded sharp and unkind. "You're always seeing people who aren't there."

"It's our fault," her father said, sounding weary. "We overeducated her to compensate for her infirmity. Her imagination gets overheated."

Lynnet wrung her hands, hoping to find the words to convince her parents.

"This is real, Father. There were three of them. I only heard a few words, but they talked of chaos in the kingdom."

"Who were these men?" her father asked. "Were they Norman or Saxon? If they're Saxon, I might join them."

He emitted a bitter, mocking laugh.

Lynnet could see her oversized mother bearing down on him as her petite father cringed back into his chair.

"Husband, do not speak those words, even in jest."

Lynnet tried to divert her mother's attention.

"Their accents were Norman. Although they used no names, I'd recognize their voices. They must be of some consequence. They wore armor."

Her mother turned away from her cringing father to confront Lynnet. Planting her fists on her hips, she made a formidable opponent outlined by candlelight. Lynnet could feel the anger pouring out of her.

"Don't get us embroiled in politics."

"She's right, Daughter." Her intellectual father's voice was conciliatory.

"Speak no more of this," her mother insisted. "It's hard enough for Saxons these days. Don't make matters worse."

Chapter Two

Lynnet was locking her chamber door for a midmorning visit with Matilda when she heard heavy boots running towards her. Before she could react, a smelly, masculine hand clasped over her mouth. Two more strong hands imprisoned her arms behind her back.

"Grab her legs. The little vixen kicked me."

"I'll knock her out. It'll be easier to wrap her in the rug."

A fist struck underneath Lynnet's chin, making her teeth rattle together and threatening to slam the insides of her head into the bony walls of her skull. The pain was horrendous before blackness descended.

The sheriff had been working up a sweat since dawn. In the wee hours, he had commandeered a scribe and two muscled retainers from the king's Tower staff. Rather than just overseeing the workers as most sheriffs would do, he pitched in to shift the weighty crates and barrels.

He liked putting his muscled body to the test and felt a camaraderie with these men. As a boy, he unloaded provisions from carts for an Ipswich innkeeper. The work reminded him of his youth and of his tavern barmaid mother, whom he still saw occasionally. On top of that, the Saxon beauty had been on his mind frequently since yesterday. While still smarting from his abrupt dismissal, he had trouble getting those blind light-blue eyes out of his thoughts. Working up a sweat while counting supplies kept him occupied enough to forget—occasionally.

Receiving this commission was a complete surprise. When summoned by the king yesterday morning, Basil expected chastisement. Relief had flooded through him when he realized his latest brawl with his wealthy half-brother would not land him in his own jail. Although Basil's post as Sheriff of London bespoke the political power of his father, the Earl of Chester, Basil knew his illegitimacy would put him on the losing side in a face-off with his vindictive half-brother, his father's legitimate, youngest son.

Stopping the thievery would be a challenge. This London residence and fortress was built by King William only a few years after securing his rightful place as ruler of Britain. Besides the garrisoned soldiers and the Lord Chamberlain's housekeeping staff, dozens of tradesmen, craftsmen, entertainers and even farmers who slept within its walls each evening were in and out of the Tower gates many times throughout the day. Although the outer walls were heavily guarded, until now there was free movement within the walls. Basil was going to put a stop to that.

He wiped the sweat from his face with his sleeve.

Starting at one end of the cellar and slowly working towards the other, he had inventoried the king's provisions to establish what was being stolen, when they were taken, and just how much was taken. He would repeat these inventories frequently to discover the pattern behind the thefts. His spies were out in the markets looking for the foodstuffs being sold there.

Basil smiled grimly.

I'll get to the bottom of these thefts!

ꟹ

Lynnet gradually recovered her senses. She willed the cobwebs to disappear from her throbbing head. Hearing scurrying sounds she suspected as being rats, Lynnet decided she must be in the cellars again. No other sounds penetrated the cold, dank atmosphere. Her attackers were gone.

Because she was not already dead, she decided the conspirators had probably secreted her here until they could transport her out of the Tower, perhaps hidden in some peddler's cart. Or was she already smuggled out?

Her stomach clenched and she prayed she was still in the Tower. She'd have a better chance of surviving. She wondered if the sheriff had anything to do with her present misfortune. Anger built in her belly and its warmth spread outward.

God rot their entrails.

Ignoring a throbbing head and restricted breathing, Lynnet struggled against her bindings, but made little headway at loosening them. Her body was bound tightly in the putrid-smelling rug the attacker had thrown around her. The rough cloth pressed against her face and fastened her arms snugly to her sides, restricting her down to her toes. Lynnet decided to roll herself out of it.

She rolled to her right, but good fortune eluded her. Lynnet rolled the opposite way and felt relieved when the dirty, mildewed rug layered off her. She sneezed, blowing away dust caked under her nose.

"I'm fortunate they didn't fasten it with cords," she mumbled to herself as she checked her bearings.

Darkness surrounded her. No lit torches gave her an

inkling as to direction.

She pushed herself free of the rug and stumbled to her feet, reaching out with searching hands. No walls were nearby.

"They must have dumped me in the middle of the room."

Lynnet shivered in the damp coldness. She wore only a lightweight, morning dress. Upon leaving her bedchamber, she had expected to be quickly sitting in front of Matilda's warming fire.

She wondered how long she'd been unconscious as she brushed herself off. Her body gave her no indication. It was neither thirsty nor hungry.

"That's a good sign. I haven't been unconscious for long."

Slowly, she slid her feet across the stone floor. Her extended hands moved left and right, up and down. When her toe struck a wooden crate, she edged her way around it and passed two more stacked crates until she felt the wall. She inched her way along, working herself past bags of foodstuffs and crates until at last she came to a door.

"You'd better be unlocked," she threatened the door.

When she found the latch, she pressed it eagerly and it clicked open.

They didn't bar the door! How stupid. Do they think blind means helpless?

She touched the silver chain around her neck and worked her fingers along its length until she reached the crystal pendant. This good luck charm must get her to safety before her kidnappers returned.

Lynnet pushed the door further open and listened. No footsteps. No voices. But she could smell foul water. She wrinkled her nose.

That stench must be the Thames. All the garbage of London

ends up in that river.

Lynnet decided she was in an outside corridor instead of an interior one. She could see vague shadows from sunlight filtering through archers' slits. She smiled, grimly, relieved to still be within Tower walls.

As she turned to her right, she caught a glimpse of a shadowy figure, beckoning. The sounds of the river came from that direction. Her grandmother's benevolent spirit was guiding her through the power of the crystal.

"I must be close to the Water Gate."

This gate opened onto the River Thames. It welcomed commerce and prisoners alike.

"The guards stationed there will take me to my chambers."

Making sure her fingers stayed connected with the massive stones of the wall, she walked towards the apparition. Although it dissolved as she got closer, Lynnet was unafraid. This kind of thing had been happening to her since she was blinded. Her parents became angry when she mentioned the apparition. She'd learned long ago not to speak of its appearances.

"Halt. Who goes there?"

A Tower guard? So soon? She was closer than she realized to the Water Gate.

"I'm lost. Help me."

The guard took her arm to steady her.

"What happened to you? You're hurt."

Lynnet touched her face, which felt sore and swollen.

"Should I take you to your family?" he asked.

After last night's humiliation, Lynnet craved the comfort of someone who listened with loving concern instead of criticism. She didn't want to be alone or to be with her parents. She wanted a chance to lay out what she overheard yesterday in the light of a friend's levelheadedness. She wanted to explain the terror of being kidnapped today. Lynnet wanted to be with her friend.

"I'm trying to reach the chambers of Lady Matilda, wife of the Baron Geoffrey de la Werreiur."

With Matilda's wool cloak covering her, Lynnet huddled on a stool, finishing a mug of heated ale and nibbling on sweetmeats. The ointment Matilda applied to heal the bruising caused by the blow to her chin also soothed pain. A roaring fire seeped warmth into her bones.

Lord Geoff's status demanded the best of apartments, even though Matilda was Anglo-Saxon. Their chamber was only a few doors from her own and that of her parents.

She and Matilda had met only a couple of weeks ago here at winter court. Soon, like soul mates, they were spilling their hearts' inner secrets to each other. She'd just finished chronicling what happened to her since yesterday.

Lynnet took another sweetmeat, indulging herself, now that she was safe and warm.

Matilda's body created a silhouette against the wall from the flickering firelight as she paced. As she turned to Lynnet, her friend's torment spilled outward.

"You must tell the authorities."

"The sheriff might be a part of this."

"I can't believe that," Geoff said, his voice getting louder as he made his point. "I've known Basil for at least five years. He's honorable."

Lynnet turned towards Geoff. He was leaning against a tapestried wall near the fireplace. Even the vague outline of his lithe, powerful body seemed ready to spring into action.

"He came along immediately afterward," she said. "He sounded angry that he'd missed those men."

"I'm sure there's a reasonable explanation."

"You must ask Basil for protection." Matilda waved her arms while making her point. "Those men are trying to kill you."

"I don't know for sure that today was connected to yesterday in the cellars. The men today were ruffians. They may have wanted ransom."

"It's more likely the two are connected," Geoff said.

"At least you believe me. My parents think I'm hearing things. Since I lost my sight, strange things sometimes happen."

Lynnet touched her crystal where it nestled under her blue woolen bodice.

Matilda gave Lynnet a hug before plopping down in a chair opposite the fireplace.

"Of course, we believe you."

Geoff moved away from the wall and approached Lynnet.

"If there's the slightest chance of trouble brewing, the sheriff needs to know. The crown must be protected."

"That's right," Matilda said.

"Basil has the king's trust," Geoff added.

"You should give him yours," Matilda insisted.

Lynnet's head was a whirl. Bewildered, she started sputtering.

"But...but...his voice..."

"Many guests from northern shires stay at the king's residences during winter court," Matilda cautioned her, "including Basil's father. They could easily sound alike."

Lynnet felt immediately relieved. Basil's appearance in the

cellar could have been pure coincidence.

"Do you think the earl could be the conspirator?" Lynnet asked.

Geoff shook his head in a shadowy movement.

"The earl would never turn against his king. But there are others from Chester who would."

The heaviness surrounding Lynnet's heart since yesterday lifted. The bond she'd immediately felt with Basil hadn't been misplaced. Her heart had known him innocent even while her mind thought him guilty.

"You must tell Basil. If the king is in danger, there must be no delay." Geoff was adamant. His certainty was like the tide. It could not be fought.

"I'll talk with the sheriff."

"You must tell your parents, also."

Lynnet turned in the direction of Matilda.

"Must I?"

Her stomach knotted at the thought of it.

"It'll be worse if you don't."

"But they told me not to get involved in politics."

"You have no choice. The king must be protected."

"You're right, of course." Lynnet was resigned.

"We'll go with you."

"From now on," Geoff said, "don't go anywhere by yourself. It's too dangerous."

Lynnet agreed. Her world was definitely no longer safe.

Basil bent over the large oak table in an anteroom of the Treasury on the storeroom level of the Tower, going over the figures the scribe had written down and double-checking the tally. A map of the cellars cross-referenced to lists of supplies in each storeroom was spread out on the table. The scribe and the retainers who had helped take the inventory were seated nearby.

When the Treasury door crashed open, Basil turned towards it, exasperated at an interruption. Only minutes before, according to a two-hour rotation schedule, the guards assigned to the vault changed with much stamping of feet and shouting of orders. Basil had just refocused on the inventory figures when here was another interruption. He turned towards the intruder, frowning. His frown changed to a smile when he saw who it was.

"Lord Geoffrey, good to see you." He shoved his wooden chair backward, scraping it across the stone floor, and rose to greet his friend with a bear hug and much slapping of backs.

"And I, you. It's been awhile."

Basil offered him a chair, but Geoff chose to stand.

"What brings you to the bowels of the Tower?"

"Lady Lynnet of Osfrith."

Basil's stomach turned queasy.

"What does she want?"

"It's a confidential matter of some urgency. I'll take you to her."

"You rich people don't care what important work you interrupt, do you?"

Geoff chuckled.

"We like to keep you poor bastards downtrodden."

Basil shook his head wearily, resigned to not completing the verification of the inventory. At the same time, his heart beat faster as he wondered how the Saxon beauty would treat him today.

Basil waved a hand towards the cluttered table.

"Give me a moment to finish up here."

He addressed the scribe and the retainers. "Lock the map and lists in the trunk. Give the guard the key. Meet me here tomorrow at dawn so we can finish the tally."

He stuck his short sword into its sheath and turned to Geoff.

"Lead on, Baron. Let's find out why the lady raised this hue and cry."

Basil sympathized with Lynnet as she stumbled over her tongue while relating the events of yesterday and this morning. Her she-devil mother butted in, criticizing and belittling.

He was also incensed.

She should have told me this yesterday. I need to report this to the king.

They were assembled in her parents' chamber. It was one of the more elegantly furnished chambers in the Tower with heavy velvet bed draperies, brightly colored tapestries and leather chairs. The large fireplace was well-stocked with logs against the chill of a bleak November day.

Lord Geoffrey and he leaned against the wall beneath the shuttered window. Lady Matilda and Lady Lynnet sat on chairs. Lady Durwyn sat primly on the edge of the bed, her feet on a stepping stool. The position put her higher than the other women. Her husband had pulled a cushioned stool towards the bed and sat like a whipped cur at his wife's feet.

Lady Lynnet had just finished relating this morning's abduction when her mother broke in.

"You must forgive my daughter, Sheriff. She's given to flights of fancy."

Lady Durwyn rose and faced him. She took a deep breath and pulled herself up to her full height.

"It's difficult for me to divulge this, but for the longest time our daughter told us she could see the ghost of my deceased mother-in-law."

"But, Mother," Lynnet said, wringing her hands, a deep frown creasing her forehead. "Lord Geoffrey found the rug they wrapped me in."

"I don't deny you were kidnapped, Daughter," her mother said in a tone that clearly said 'do not interrupt'. "The bruising on your face is serious, not to speak of unsightly."

Lynnet visibly winced.

"I just say you were taken for ransom, not conspiracy. After all, the wool trade made my lands prosperous. I'm quite wealthy. Any fool knows those ruffians were after our money."

Lynnet blushed, looking embarrassed. Basil was about to come to her defense when her father spoke up.

"My dear, we need to keep an open mind."

Lord Wilfgive's high-pitched, tenor voice seemed excessively conciliatory. In size, Lynnet's father was only a couple of inches taller than his daughter. His wife towered over both. Despite his well-known reputation as a scholar, on the short-legged stool he seemed insignificant. The exception was the quality of his clothing. That was designed to impress.

"We should hear what the sheriff has to say," Lord Geoffrey said.

Everyone's attention focused on Basil. When Lady Lynnet turned towards where he stood, his heart speeded up despite his intention to be disinterested. He cleared his throat.

"I'm investigating a series of robberies."

His bass voice reverberated against the stone walls, making

him self-conscious. This was the aspect of his occupation he liked the least. A man of action, words were a second choice.

"It's possible this abduction had nothing to do with yesterday. Perhaps the thieves saw your daughter as an easy prey for kidnapping and a ransom."

Geoff pushed himself abruptly away from the wall, seeming to startle Lynnet. He ran his fingers through his hair as if agitated.

"But she heard someone speak of chaos in the kingdom. We can't take lightly anything that touches on the king."

Before Basil could assure Geoff that action would be taken, her father spoke up.

"You haven't known us long, Baron. Our daughter hears voices that no others hear. It started after illness caused her blindness."

Basil watched Lynnet's face flush beet-red.

"Father, I'm blind, not deaf. My hearing is better than yours. Most times, what I hear can be explained."

"But there are other times, Daughter. This may be one of them."

Basil's stomach gave a twist as if he was the one under attack. Lynnet was being made to look foolish in front of her friends and him. He cleared his throat.

"I'll look into both your daughter's kidnapping and the conspiracy," he assured them.

Geoff leaned back against the wall as if satisfied.

Lady Durwyn started pacing, something a noble woman never did in company. The train of her purple woolen kirtle dragged against the flagstones. It demonstrated the intensity of her distress as she spoke.

"I don't want to be embroiled in lengthy investigations."

“I’ll do my best to shield you during my inquiries.”

The husband calmed his wife, his voice soothing.

“See, my dear, the sheriff will handle everything. We don’t have to be involved.”

Not involved? Your own daughter’s life is at stake.

Chapter Three

Basil stood at attention in an antechamber of the Great Hall of Westminster Palace. He felt naked without his dagger and short sword, but no man came before the king wearing weapons, not even the sheriff. The arms were left with the guard before entering the antechamber door. The arched windows were shuttered against the chill of this November day. Candles set in wall sconces provided flickering light to the small chamber.

The king sat behind a carved table in a wooden chair whose curved arms ended in cat paws. Hanging on the wall behind the king was purple silk, draping nearly ceiling to floor. An ornate shield hung to the left side. A mace and battle-axe crisscrossed on the right.

King Henry was renowned for building his bureaucracy with men plucked from obscurity instead of appointing contentious barons. These were educated men from the working class or noble sons not in line to inherit. The corrupt civil servants inherited from his brother, King Rufus, were gradually being replaced by men the king could trust.

King Henry certainly plucked me out of obscurity.

Basil's first ten years were lived in an Ipswich tavern near the docks where his mother was a barmaid. The raucous, rowdy sailors and travelers going to and coming from France were all he knew until his father decided to acknowledge the bastard son he conceived one night before sailing to Normandy. Yanking Basil away from his mother's care, the earl dropped him into the academic life of a Chester monastery.

Since the earl was their benefactor, Basil could always be forgiven indiscretions by monks who wanted nothing to stop the flow of money from their patron. After seven years of Latin, Greek, French, Math, Science, Astronomy, Music and Literature, he was removed again without notice and thrust into training as a military officer. This life suited him. There was nothing he liked better than to knock a few heads together when men got in the way of his justice.

Basil shifted his bulk self-consciously as hooded, dark eyes, hovering above a long, beaked nose, concealed King Henry's cunning and intelligence. He seemed to take his sheriff's measure. The sheriff silently vowed to live up to the deeds of his namesake, St. Basil the Great. It wasn't wise to disappoint a powerful king.

"You're the best man to investigate," the king's deputy was saying, "especially if Normans are involved as Lady Lynnet believes. You're a man who knows his duty."

The king leaned forward. "I'm told you are not open to bribery."

"No man will succeed in avoiding the king's justice by trying to bribe me."

His throat felt tighter than usual, making his voice higher. It came from not being entirely at ease in exalted company.

Basil was glad for his years of training in the monastery. The monks had given him the words, at least, to hold his own in polite company. His mother's contribution to his vocabulary tended towards the coarse language of the wharves.

"I want the truth, no matter where it leads." The king

slowly shook his head, looking troubled. “These days, it’s hard to tell friend from foe.”

King Henry relaxed back into his chair. From his manner, it was obvious the meeting was over.

Basil relaxed his own stance in response.

The deputy took charge. A man of small stature and slight build, he had remained standing to the right of the king as if not wanting to be intimidated by Basil’s height. What Baron Otheur lacked in stature, he made up for with a booming voice and an air of authority.

“Report to me personally on your investigations. We’ll meet here midmorning two days from now.”

“Yes, my lord.”

“You are dismissed. These coins should cover expenses.”

Basil caught the leather pouch thrown by the deputy. Its weight assured him it would buy informants.

Late that night, long after Basil had returned from his meeting with the king, Matilda and Geoff were relaxing over a goblet of ale before retiring. Matilda, a shawl around her, snuggled her head into Geoff’s chest as they sat side-by-side on a bench at the table in their bedchamber. His arm hung around her shoulder, his right hand caressing the curve of her breast. She twisted slightly to give him more access.

“I had no idea Lynnet’s parents dealt so harshly with her,” he said.

“She talked a little about it. Until you listen to them, it’s hard to comprehend. My parents were always so loving towards me.”

She smiled contentedly as Geoff brushed back unruly, red-blond tresses and planted warm kisses on her forehead.

"As we will be towards our children."

Geoff pushed the shawl away to gain access to the swell of her breast.

"She needs a friend," Matilda said as excited tingles ran through her body. Warmth developed in her loins. "She's very close to her companion, but Evelyn can't protect her from her parents."

"Understandable," Geoff said as he cuddled and nuzzled her neck. "She's hired help."

"I'm going to keep my eye on Lynnet. May I invite her to our manor early next year?"

"Certainly. We'll help her any way we can." His hand slipped down to caress between her legs.

Matilda lifted her head and put her arms around his neck. She kissed his bearded face.

"Let's go to bed."

The next day, Lynnet rested her fingers lightly on Matilda's linen-clad arm as they made their way to the Great Hall for midday meal. She hoped to identify the men in the cellar or her kidnappers by their voices.

"The noise in a castle this size always surprises me," she said. "At home, we're as quiet as church mice compared to this place."

"I know. Besides the king's guests, there's a whole garrison of soldiers quartered here."

"Not to speak of the tradesmen daily in and out."

"And the retainers whose families live within the walls. I don't envy Basil his task of finding thieves and kidnappers among this crowd."

Footsteps approached and Matilda was saying, "Good day,

sirs."

Two male voices answered. When they were out of range, Matilda asked, "What about them?"

Lynnet shook her head. "They aren't the ones."

"They were soldiers. Here comes the cloth merchant. Some gentlewoman must want a new gown for the holidays."

The process again was unfruitful.

"I'm open to adventures," Matilda said quietly, "but what we're trying is risky. Dangerous even."

Lynnet's face still carried the bruises.

"I won't be safe until I can identify those men and take their names to the king. It's just as dangerous to sit twiddling my thumbs, waiting on a sheriff who's dragging his feet because he's been told by my parents it's all my imagination."

"Basil's not so easily swayed."

"You may bow out if you wish."

"Never."

They met no one on the spiral staircase, but as they drew near to the crowded Hall, the level of noise increased dramatically.

"Most of the seats above the salt have already been claimed."

Since Matilda was wife to a Norman baron pledged to the king, she had high status in seating at the table. Lynnet was her equal. Only her family's Anglo-Saxon heritage detracted from her worthiness.

And my blindness, of course.

"The king's not here. We can't be seated yet," Matilda said. "Suppose we put our cloaks on the bench to reserve two spaces. Then, we'll walk around so you can listen to voices."

"Fine."

Lynnet allowed Matilda to lead her to the table. The Great Hall was lit by many candles, torches and fireplaces so she could make out shapes of guests and furnishings.

Lynnet unclasped the lightweight cloak used to keep away the chill of drafty corridors and draped it over a bench that Matilda said was as close to the head table as they could get today because of their late arrival.

That done, Lynnet allowed Matilda to lead her around the Hall. Sliding her soft-soled slippers across cold pavement stones disturbed the rushes and released their aroma.

"The rushes must be fresh. The air is less foul today."

"Wait until tonight after the king's hounds leave droppings all day."

Lynnet noticed they were pausing near groups of men. Matilda's hands were flying about her face as she supposedly described tapestries and metal work on armor and battle instruments. Should anyone overhear, the low-voiced recitation about color and design masked their real purpose.

"Pretending to be knowledgeable about Norman art, are you?"

Lynnet cringed at the icy disdain directed towards Matilda in the woman's voice.

"No pretending. Your brother instructed me on the origin of the hangings."

"And who is this?"

"My friend, Lady Lynnet of Osfrith."

"Another Saxon," she said with disgust. Lynnet heard the woman turn and walk away.

"Who was that? She's awful."

"That's my arrogant sister-in-law."

"How unfortunate for you."

"Lady Rosamund is estranged from her brother because of our marriage. She never approaches when Geoff's around, but delights in hurting my feelings when I'm on my own."

"It would be a blessing if she stayed away altogether."

"No chance. Her status-seeking husband comes around trying to wheedle his way back into Geoff's good graces."

"It must be difficult for you."

"It is. She believes Normans are superior and is furious with her brother for marrying me."

I wonder if Basil has any such arrogant relatives.

Lynnet strained to pick out and analyze each male voice in the vicinity, searching for those she heard discussing conspiracy.

"So many men's voices, but none I can identify."

Despite the number of men in attendance from all walks of life, Lynnet matched not a one of them to the voices she heard in the basement nor to yesterday's kidnappers.

"The king's arriving with his daughter," Matilda said. "We have to sit down or become conspicuous."

"It's so discouraging."

"Maybe it's better that you stop trying."

It was near midnight as Basil wended his way through dark and dingy London streets. He wore a dirty, ripped, brown tunic to blend in with his surroundings. Baggy workman's pants, tied at the waist by cord, held weapons, not tools, in the pockets. His hand rested on the hilt of a highly sharpened throwing knife. His ears stayed alert for sounds that would give away the stealth of a mugger as he strode towards the lighted doorway of Hanged Man Tavern.

He was meeting Nicolas, the leader of his band of London spies. Their discussions tonight would start the investigation of his second commission from the king—discovering if there was truth to what Lady Lynnet overheard.

Basil stepped over the tavern's high, wide, wooden doorsill, built to keep out rainwater rushing through the street from higher elevations to the Thames only blocks away. Only a few tallow candles pushed away the darkness of the common room. Snores rose from travelers paying to sleep within the safety of tavern walls. The ancient wood reeked of a hundred years of unwashed bodies and smoky fires.

The landlord saw him enter and gestured for Basil to follow him up the creaky stairs to a small, dark room at the end of the corridor. The single candle on the table revealed that the informant had already arrived.

Money exchanged hands and the landlord bowed his way out of the room, closing the heavy door securely behind him. Theirs was an association both found beneficial.

"Good e'en, Sheriff," the spy said.

Nicolas wore faded clothing and a hang-dog look. Small of stature and of wiry build, the nondescript informant blended easily into crowds. Anyone passing him on the street would take him for an indentured apprentice, brow beaten, insignificant.

Basil knew better. The man was quick witted, a survivor of rough-and-tumble streets and wise enough to know how and when to blend in instead of standing out. He knew the man was hired by nobility and must have accumulated a hoard of money for his services. Even the funds disbursed during the short time Basil was sheriff would give this informant a comfortable living. Still, he looked like he'd lived most of the time on the streets.

"Good eventide to you, my friend."

Basil slapped the man on his back in hearty greeting before

pulling up a stool to sit down. Since Basil's own roots were in the rough dock areas of Ipswich, he was comfortable sitting down with the ragtag Nicolas. He placed his throwing knife on the scarred and wobbly table.

"I was surprised to get your summons," the informant said. "I've not yet gleaned news on the thefts."

Nicolas took a gulp of the ale the landlord provided for their meeting. Basil lifted the cracked pitcher and poured a mug full for himself. He stretched out his legs and made himself comfortable.

"There's a new problem. A possible plot against the king. I need to know who's behind it."

"By my troth, I'll find them if I have to sniff through every gutter in London."

"We may not find what we need in the gutters," Basil said. "The men wore armor."

The sheriff related Lynnet's story.

"Those are the words she believes she overheard," Basil said. "There's doubt because her parents claim that she sometimes hears voices that no one else hears."

Basil had felt Lady Lynnet's pain at her parents' dismissal of her words. Yet, he had to let his chief spy know there was a possibility all this had no more substance than a puff of smoke.

"Better to keep the king safe," Nicolas said. "Our informants won't mind a wild goose chase as long as they get paid."

The sheriff removed a moderate-size, leather bag of coins from his pocket and placed it with a clunk between them on the table.

"You'll all be paid. The usual up front. The rest when the information can be validated."

“We’ll need to infiltrate the barracks.”

“Agreed.” Basil leaned forward, intense.

“Overlook no one. Question servants and merchants of the wealthy. Find out what messages are being carried between them, what conversations overheard.”

“You can trust me to protect the king.”

Basil leaned back to give his final order.

“Investigate Saxon and Norman alike.”

Chapter Four

Two mornings later, Lynnet was on her way to visit Matilda. For protection, she brought Evelyn, her personal servant, companion and reader.

Lynnet knew each step by heart and could have walked it alone, but today she had something on her mind. Not wanting injury from a distracted step, she placed her hand lightly on Evelyn's shoulder.

"The bruising on your face has gone down, my lady. Does your chin still hurt?"

"Occasionally."

"I'll be glad when we can leave this evil place," Evelyn said in a wistful tone.

"I long for the sweet smell of meadow grasses myself. I long to get the stink of town garbage out of my nostrils."

Evelyn clucked her tongue. "Your parents should get you out of London. They should speak to the king and explain the circumstances of an early journey home."

"They won't. They don't want to embroil themselves in controversy. They want to maintain the status quo."

Their selfishness worked in Lynnet's favor. Leaving the court early created a different problem. Her parents would force her that much sooner into marriage with a man who wanted her money and family status, not her.

Yet, finding a husband to love in London seemed increasingly dismal. Evil doers lurking in corridors made looking for a husband well nigh impossible.

Too bad Basil is unsuitable.

Evelyn knocked on Matilda's door. When it swung open, Lynnet saw the grayed outline of her friend, silhouetted by the winter sun streaming through the windows.

"Lynnet! What a wonderful surprise."

"Good morning, Matilda. I hope I'm not intruding."

"Not at all. Geoff's gone to an assembly and won't be back for hours. I'm in the mood for company."

Lynnet dismissed Evelyn as Matilda ushered her into the chamber. After the door swung closed, she heard a bar fall into place, locking the door.

"Make yourself at home. There's a stool by the fireplace if that's all right."

"A stool will do nicely."

"Do you want anything to eat?"

"No food, but I would accept ale."

Lynnet made her way carefully towards the light of the fireplace. Her foot touched the wooden leg of a stool before she realized she was so close. She bent, her hands gliding over the wooden surface, determining its size and height, then sat down. When she heard Matilda coming, she reached out and her friend slipped a wooden goblet into her hand. She sat, sipping the sweet ale.

"So tell me, what brought you to see me at such an early hour."

"I haven't heard from the sheriff for two days. I don't think he's doing anything about my kidnapping."

"He may not have anything to report," Matilda said soothingly.

"At least, he could let me know he's trying."

"He's probably too busy."

"I think he's dragging his feet."

"I'm sure Basil's not dragging his feet."

Defense of her friend resonated in Matilda's voice.

Lynnet shrugged her shoulders.

"What Norman sheriff is going to put Normans in jail to protect an Anglo-Saxon, especially three rich enough to own armor?"

"Basil would."

Lynnet winced at the vigor behind her friend's defense of the Norman sheriff. She had nothing against Basil personally. In point of fact, he'd been pleasantly on her mind fairly continuously these past two days.

"I'm just saying he has a commission from the king. Why should he take time to bother about my kidnapping?"

"Because he said he would. I'm married to a Norman. They are men of honor too."

Matilda sounded angry.

"I don't mean to offend. It's just that I understand how things work, and they don't necessarily work in favor of Anglo-Saxons."

"So you're not against Basil himself?"

"Definitely not. Actually, I've been wondering about him. I wonder what he looks like."

"Basil? A rugged brute."

Matilda's voice carried admiration despite the derogatory description.

"What do you mean?"

"Basil's not a polished courtier. He's a man of action. Even violence."

Lynnet remembered the pressure on her arm when he grabbed it in the cellars.

"He has ebony black hair, a long, straight, dominant nose, a mustache, and a beard he keeps closely cropped. With thick, black eyebrows, he constantly looks dark and stormy."

Lynnet pictured Basil's face. If the opportunity arose, she would trace that bearded jaw.

"His eyes remind me of King Henry's, dark and piercing, the kind of eyes that make scoundrels shake in their boots."

Lynnet set her goblet on the floor under the stool so that she wouldn't accidentally spill it.

"You make him sound terrifying."

Matilda laughed.

"To his enemies, yes."

All her life Lynnet had been around a dominant mother and a docile father. While she picked up much of her independence from her fierce mother, she had no example for an aggressive male.

"You'd love his hands," Matilda said. "They're broad and angular. Very capable. A lot like Geoff's. And, oh, the things Geoff can do with his hands."

Lynnet imagined Basil's hands on her and a heated flush rose.

Matilda laughed.

"Look at you. You're blushing. I'll have to dust off my

matchmaking skills and get you two hitched up."

Count Courbet de Shereborne sprawled on a massive, carved, wooden chair in his bedchamber, his leg draped over one arm of the chair, a goblet of wine lazily held in his right hand. Count Maximilian de Selsey sat in an opposite chair, nibbling from a plate of precisely lined up chunks of cheese. Sir André de Chester slouched against the wall near the fireplace, his wine goblet resting on the mantel, his facial expression reflecting the consternation evident in his voice.

"I'd feel safer if I knew she wasn't ever going to open her lying Saxon mouth."

"She already has," Maximilian said. "My wife is sister to Lady Matilda's husband. I bribed a castle servant for gossip. Although Lady Lynnet talked, no one believes her. Her parents told the sheriff she's always seeing things and hearing voices that aren't there."

André threw his head back and laughed heartily. "God's mercy. Providence is on our side!"

"I don't know. Someone might believe her," Courbet said.

"I do know," Maximilian continued, "that my wretched Anglo-Saxon sister-in-law is accompanying that woman everywhere to make sure she's not attacked again. She thinks it was a kidnapping for ransom."

André moaned.

"If you keep your mouth shut when she's near," Maximilian said, "we'll have nothing to fear. She may be able to identify our voices, but she certainly can't identify us by sight."

Courbet slammed the silver wine goblet onto the floor beside his chair and started to pace the room, running his fingers through his blond hair. "We need to be certain she's no risk," he said, his temper flaring.

"How?" Andre asked. "Our last plan failed. She has more protection now."

Maximilian turned to André.

"Her parents say she sees ghosts. We'll make everyone think she's gone mad. They won't know if what she hears is real or imagined."

"How?"

"I'll make sure her personal servant turns ill," Maximilian said. "I'll substitute my own servant, one generously compensated to make the lady think she's touched in the head. We'll have her soon believing that we were part of an overwrought imagination."

Courbet stopped pacing and stared at Maximilian. *The little bastard is devious.*

"Her parents will bundle her off to home," Maximilian said. "She'll be out of our hair."

"Count me in."

"Me too."

Chapter Five

Dispirited, Basil sat in the rundown tavern room and mulled over the lack of progress made the last two days. The Tower's storage rooms were organized according to who would be using the supplies. The rooms were then padlocked and the duplicate key given to the steward in charge. The originals were held under the close eye of the guards in the Treasury Room.

Trusted spies out among staff and soldiers listened for any hint of trouble. So far the effort had proved fruitless, but his best informant was due at any moment. Posing as a messenger, the man overheard a great deal of information useful to Basil with no one the wiser. The footsteps coming down the hallway were probably his.

The door, slightly ajar, opened slowly and Nicolas stuck in his head.

Basil waved him in.

"Lock the door behind you."

When the informant was seated and ale was poured, Basil asked, "What's the news?"

Nicolas got right to the point.

"There's a rumor about dissatisfaction among some Norman nobility with the amount of political power being transferred into the hands of the Anglo-Saxons."

Basil's stomach lurched. Nicolas was confirming his worst fears. He hated the murky mire of politics. He dealt more easily with crimes of passion or pure violence.

"Go on."

"Some thought when the queen died that the king would come to his senses and stop trying to appease the Saxons."

"What do they think he should do?"

"They feel the only way to rule is by force. Ruthlessly suppress any rebellion they instigate."

"And if they aren't rebelling?"

"Then make it appear as if they are."

"God rot their entrails."

Basil pounded his fist so hard on the table the goblets of ale rattled.

He'd grown up believing Saxons inferior. These past days, seeing the gentility and intelligence of Lady Lynnet, his attitude was changing. He didn't want Anglo-Saxons quashed. His duty to the king was to protect them, if innocent.

"These men are antagonistic to Saxons, but are they loyal to the king?"

"To the extent that he holds the crown," Nicolas said before taking another gulp of ale. "I heard no rumors of treason. They are just trying to make it look as if Saxons are behind the beatings and robberies of the king's tax collectors in the parishes and the thefts in the Tower."

"Who are these grumblers?"

If they could be named, Basil could collect evidence against them and close this investigation quickly, thus taking Lady Lynnet out of harm's way.

"No names. I only know that they're Norman nobility."

Basil grimaced, feeling as if a powerful black hand squeezed his heart. A cold morning wind blew, finding access through the cracks in the wall. It seemed to portend problems ahead.

A great deal of his success as sheriff derived from the goodwill of the Norman barons flocking to London in the king's service. The last thing he needed was to investigate them. Still, it was his duty and he would not shirk it.

Basil paid Nicolas and sent him on his way. Alone, he relentlessly paced the dingy room, his hands clasped behind his back and his head hung low in troubled thought.

Here was confirmation that what Lynnet overheard was not just her imagination. On top of that, the men in the basement were not soldiers, but noblemen. Men of power. Men with money to spend to achieve their own ends.

"That female may have stumbled into a hornet's nest."

Late that night, Lynnet pounded on her friend's door loud enough to wake them should they be sleeping. Within a short period of time, the door was pulled open.

"Lynnet, what are you doing here at this hour?"

"Why are you alone?" Geoff asked.

"I'm sorry. I know it's late. I've been waiting up for Evelyn to help me prepare for bed. I just got word she's been taken violently ill from eating bad food. It will be at least a week before she can return to her duties."

"How terrible."

"The man from the chamberlain's staff who brought the news says a new servant will arrive in the morning, but I need some help tonight."

"You poor dear," Matilda said.

"My parents are long asleep and their servants dismissed. Besides, I'd rather not wake them and encourage another 'I told you so' lecture. Can you be a good friend and loan me your servant for tonight?"

"I'll do better than that," Matilda said. "I'll come help you myself."

"Are you certain you understand what to do?"

Maximilian was speaking to the servant girl lounging against his bedchamber wall. Her voluptuous curves were blatantly displayed by a low neckline and a cinched-in waist. A sassy thing, he thought. He'd occasionally bedded her with pleasure.

"Not only do I understand, but it'll be fun."

"I'll keep her personal servant sick as long as possible, but you'll have to work fast. The apothecary is in my pay. He's feeding her small amounts of poison and diagnosing the results as eating bad food. There's only so long we can stretch this out without raising suspicion."

"Don't worry. I can handle it."

"You're sure?"

"I handle you all right, don't I?" She placed her hands on her broad hips and threw her head back provocatively. Maximilian ignored her.

"I've arranged for you to take the servant's place starting this morning."

"I'll be ready."

"Do you think you can convince the lady she's going mad within a week's time?"

She flipped her loose, curly black hair back from her face with her hand.

"Give me that stack of coins we agreed upon and I'll make certain of it."

"Have you worked with a blind person before this?" Lynnet asked the woman.

"No, my lady."

"Until my companion recovers, you'll need to do a great many services for me. I do as much as I can on my own, but there are certain things I cannot do."

"I'll do my best, my lady."

"There are rules. For one thing, don't move furniture around. I've memorized where everything is placed in this room. I'll walk into it if something is moved. Is that understood?"

"Yes, my lady."

"You'll need to help me cut up my food and handle hot drinks."

"Yes, my lady."

"I will break my fast now."

"Yes, my lady. I'll bring food from the kitchens. I'll only be a short time."

Lynnet paced her bedchamber. She was getting increasingly annoyed.

"Where is that woman? I'll starve to death before she returns."

Lynnet was just about convinced her new servant was not returning, that perhaps she should follow her parents' example and go down to the Hall for her morning meal, when she heard the door open.

"Who's there?"

A shiver ran down her spine. She turned towards the door, ready to defend herself.

She'd been skittish since the kidnapping. Evelyn and her parents were trained to announce their entrances. That way she knew right away it was someone who would not hurt her.

"It's Fleur, your new maidservant."

The breath Lynnet was holding released and her straining lungs filled with air.

"Announce yourself when you enter. That way I know it's someone friendly."

"I will, my lady."

Was there sarcasm in that voice? Couldn't be. Why would Fleur chance getting caught being sarcastic and jeopardize her position? *I'm being overly sensitive.*

She heard a noise. When she turned, Fleur was bending over something.

"What was that?"

"I bumped the table. Don't worry. Your food didn't spill."

Lynnet's knees still trembled as she made her way across the chamber to sit down. She was having trouble seeing outlines.

It seems extra dark in my bedchamber this morning.

She felt along the edge of the table, wondering why the chair seemed farther away than usual. When at last she found it, she sank into it gratefully.

"What took you so long? I thought you were going to hurry."

"Long? It's only been a short while, my lady."

"Impossible. I must have waited an hour."

"You are mistaken, my lady."

Lynnet was shocked. Over the years since being blinded, she'd developed an excellent sense of time. Why would that skill fail her this morning?

Her annoyance intensified.

"Well, I won't argue about it now. Put the food down, please."

As she heard the plates of food being set out, she remembered having trouble finding the chair.

"I told you not to move the furniture around. This chair was shifted from its regular place."

"I moved nothing, my lady."

Lynnet frowned. This conversation was frustrating.

"I don't have problems finding things in my own bedchamber unless they've been moved."

"You must have moved it yourself, my lady. It was like that when I arrived this morning."

Lynnet thought her tone more saucy than subservient, but dismissed the thought as unworthy. She was comparing an untried servant to Evelyn who, over the years, had become a friend.

"I'd never do anything as stupid as that."

"Perhaps your parents moved it. You said they stopped by this morning, but decided to go down to the Hall rather than wait for my interview."

"They know better."

"I don't know what else to suggest, my lady. Why don't you relax over your meal while I straighten up the room for you?"

Lynnet touched the table in front of her. There was nothing there. Her stomach growled and churned out acid.

"Where's my food?"

"It's to your left, my lady."

"I should have told you I always eat facing the fireplace. The light makes it easier for me to make out the plates of food."

"The chamberlain told me that this morning when he gave me instructions. I placed your food facing the fireplace. I wondered why you sat in the wrong direction."

Lynnet swiveled on her chair. The fireplace was indeed to the right of her. How could she have been so stupid? Had the events of this past week gotten to her?

"Do you want me to help you get to the chair that faces the fireplace, my lady?"

"I'll do it myself," Lynnet snapped. She scowled as she stood and traced her fingers along the tabletop. Eventually, they touched her plate of food. No wonder it had seemed a long time getting to the chair. She'd been moving along the broad end of the rectangular table.

"I've cut up your food for you."

Lynnet said a grudging "thank you" as she steadied the plate with her left hand. She reached out her right hand to the food.

I could swear it is darker in here today. Eating is usually easier than this.

"Are the drapes pulled from the windows?" She thought she remembered hearing that happen as her parents were leaving her bedchamber to go for their morning meal. Now, she wasn't so sure.

"Yes, my lady. It's a dark day outside."

Lynnet frowned.

"I'll straighten the bed linen if you don't need my help with your food."

She heard her new servant make her way around the bed,

straightening bed linen and fluffing up pillows.

"What's on this plate?"

"Cheese and bread. I cut it up for you."

The cheese and bread were in tiny little cubes.

"There's no need to cut my food this small. I have no trouble swallowing."

"I'll remember that, my lady."

Lynnet reached out and picked up a grayed-out shape.

"What's in this bowl?"

"Hot porridge, my lady. Be careful you don't burn yourself. There's a small pitcher of cream to cool it down."

Lynnet found the bowl barely warm. What was that woman talking about?

"This is cold."

"I'm not surprised. You've been sitting there daydreaming such a long time."

Had her changing of chairs taken such a long time? It felt like an instant.

She picked up a piece of bread to eat with her cold porridge and found it too hard to chew.

"You've brought me the stale bread for the puddings. Be careful what you choose in the kitchens."

The servant's stopped what she was doing and came over to the table. Lynnet smelled Fleur's body perspiration as she reached in front to pick up a piece of bread and eat it.

"You're right. It's stale."

"You can believe me when I tell you it is."

"That's strange. This bread was with the others being served. Someone must have mixed up the loaves. I'll go down and get another one."

"Never mind. I'm losing my appetite." Lynnet pushed the plate away.

The new servant went back to working on the bedding as Lynnet chewed a piece of cheese.

It's a bad day in the kitchens. This cheese is almost rotten.

Before she got around to complaining, something else caught her attention.

"What's that bad odor?"

"What odor, my lady?"

"You can't smell that?"

"Your nose must be better than mine. I can't smell a thing."

"Well I do. That odor is making me sick."

The maidservant ostentatiously moved around the bedchamber looking behind and under things and obviously sniffing as she went. Lynnet sat rigidly on the chair. *Am I going to be proved wrong again in front of this new servant?*

She heard Fleur at the far side of the bed, pulling up the bed covers and dropping to her knees to look underneath.

"Here's your problem. You left the lid off your chamber pot. The bowel movement in it stinks when you get close up. I'll take this pot away and clean it for you."

Was she losing her mind?

"I haven't used the chamber pot this morning."

"You must be mistaken. There's definitely one in here," the new servant said as she replaced the lid, diminishing the odor.

"I didn't do that I tell you."

"If not you, who else?"

Lynnet's mouth clamped shut. It couldn't have been anyone else.

"I'll take this away." Fleur clucked her tongue in a manner

to broadcast her revulsion. “I can’t imagine anyone sneaking in here and leaving this behind,” she mumbled loud enough for Lynnet to overhear as she crossed the room.

Lynnet’s head pounded and her heart beat rapidly. It was ridiculous, of course. There had to be a logical explanation for the chamber pot. Perhaps she forgot she’d used it last night. After all, she’d been greatly upset when she learned Evelyn was ill. Lynnet touched her crystal.

The maid servant went out the door, forgetting to close it behind her, leaving Lynnet vulnerable.

“Fleur, close the door behind you,” she yelled.

There was an unlocking noise and she heard the hinges creak as the door was pushed open.

“What was that, my lady? I’d just closed the door when you spoke.”

Lynnet felt like she was going mad.

“Never mind. It was nothing.”

Chapter Six

"I'm sorry, Lady Lynnet, that your new servant does not please you," the chamberlain said that afternoon. He came to her chambers upon summons, after she'd decided she didn't want to go through another morning like this one. "I'm unable to provide another. Staff is short-handed. The king has many guests for winter court."

"There is no other servant?"

"None. Perhaps you can exchange servants with your parents until your own is well."

The very idea of asking her parents to make such a sacrifice chilled her down to the ends of her toes.

"I wouldn't dream of inconveniencing my parents. I suppose I'll have to make do until my own servant recovers."

Basil strode purposefully along the corridor. He was on his way to Lady Lynnet's chamber to tell her he had corroborating evidence to her conspiracy theory. A short while earlier, he informed the man guarding the lady to be suspicious of Norman noblemen. He'd arranged for another guard for the evening hours and signed letters of authorization for free passage for them anywhere in the Tower.

Just as he came abreast of Lord Geoff's chamber door, it opened and the baron stepped out. They embraced and greeted each other.

"My good friend," Geoff said, "why are you prowling these corridors? No thievery on my floor, I hope."

Basil gestured down the corridor.

"I'm on my way to Lady Lynnet's chambers. I have discovered evidence for a possible conspiracy."

A worried look crossed Lord Geoff's face.

"Who's involved?"

Basil could not reassure him.

"I have no names. Rumor has it they are Norman lords dissatisfied with the power being given to Anglo-Saxons."

"God's wounds," Geoff said. "Next thing they'll be haunting me. Matilda is Saxon."

"I know. But I think you're too closely allied to King Henry to be bothered."

Geoff grimaced.

"We're newlyweds. We're still getting to know one another. This is no time to throw political problems into the mix."

Basil acknowledged Geoff's concern with a nod. He had a Saxon woman problem of his own.

"I understand Lady Lynnet didn't believe I would follow through with an investigation."

He was surprised at how much that hurt him.

"I'm an honorable man. She should have believed me."

Geoff laid an arm across Basil's shoulders.

"Saxons haven't had good experience with Norman law. They are skeptical of anything we say. It plays havoc with a marriage."

Geoff removed his arm from Basil's shoulders and grasped his upper arms in an iron grip.

"Wait for your retaliation, my friend. She's probably in the middle of dressing for the Westminster Palace dance. Lynnet's coming with us tonight."

"She doesn't have her own escort?"

"No. We'll keep an eye on her."

Basil frowned as Geoff released his arms and stepped back. Lady Lynnet needed close watching. She'd blundered into dangerous waters. Newlyweds, enjoying a dance together, were not the most alert escorts for the lady at this critical time.

The sooner I find these carrion, the sooner she'll be safe.

"What about her parents? Will they accompany you?"

"No, thank goodness. We won't have the displeasure of their company. They don't travel at night."

"I'll escort her. After all, it's a sheriff's duty to keep citizens safe."

Geoff laughed heartily. "You said that with a straight face."

Basil grinned in spite of himself. "Spending an evening looking at a lovely woman won't be burdensome."

"Come on," Geoff said, grabbing his arm. "I'll take you over there. I want to see her reaction."

Basil knocked loudly on Lynnet's chamber door. It was cracked open by a serving wench.

"Is Lady Lynnet receiving? I'm the Sheriff of London and Lord Geoff accompanies me."

Lynnet's musical voice drifted across the chamber.

"Please come in. And welcome. Sit at table with me."

She was standing by the table with one hand touching it.

She turned in the direction of the maidservant.

"Fleur, please pour some ale for my visitors."

It was uncanny how she knew where people were positioned in a room.

Geoff pulled out a chair and dropped casually into it, saying, "I thought you'd be dressing for the dance tonight. Matilda's been driving me crazy asking what gown to wear and what accessories."

Lynnet laughed, a high, tinkling sound that Basil thought must match the voices of angels.

"There's no need for her to fuss," Geoff said. "My wife looks beautiful in anything. You will too. Why haven't you started dressing?"

"My companion is sick from bad food and the maidservant assigned to me is having trouble helping me with my clothing."

Geoff pushed his chair back and strode to the windows.

"No wonder. If she'd pull the drapes open she'd have more light to see by." He pushed the heavy drapes to one side on both windows.

"I thought they were open."

Basil thought Lynnet's face looked stricken as he sat down at the table.

"I'll choose for you," Geoff said, striding towards the wardrobe. He flung open the doors with a crash. "Lord knows I have enough experience with my wife to know what you females want."

"Most kind. I was getting frustrated."

"I brought you an escort for tonight's dance," Geoff said over his shoulder as he rummaged through the clothing. "The honorable sheriff."

Lynnet looked stunned. Basil couldn't tell if that was good

or bad for his part. He was after all a bastard son. She was second cousin to a queen. He waited anxiously for her next words.

"You're very kind, but I'd be a boring companion. I've never danced in public in London. I've danced country dances in my home parish, but I don't know if they are played here. I planned to sit and listen to the music."

Relief passed through him. The shock seen on her face had nothing to do with his circumstances, only with her own feelings of inadequacy.

Just looking at her will make the evening pass. With her being blind, Basil could look to his heart's content without making the lady ill at ease.

"Nonetheless, I would be pleased to be your escort."

Lynnet smiled brilliantly and, to Basil, it was like the sun bursting forth from behind a cloud.

"I accept. I crave something cheerful. This past week has been frightening."

Geoff broke in to describe the clothes he'd chosen. When Lynnet agreed with his choices, the men departed so she could dress.

It was only when he was almost to his own chambers that Basil realized he'd never told Lynnet his true reason for visiting her today.

Within two hours, Lynnet found herself fed, dressed and being escorted to the stables by the towering sheriff, with Matilda and Geoff walking behind. It was almost as if the afternoon visit from the sheriff, and having Lord Geoff choose her clothing, spurred Fleur to be extra proficient at getting her dressed and out the door.

She laid a gloved hand on Basil's wool-covered forearm as they waited for their horses to be saddled. His arm was satisfyingly muscled and the muscles rippled as he moved. He must have bathed recently. An aroma of soap was mixed in with those of wool, leather and horses.

"I've never ridden at night."

Her parents had trouble seeing and never traveled after dusk if they could find a way out of it. Lynnet was going to the dance in defiance of their wishes.

Basil patted her hand, his blunt, capable fingers reassuring.

"I'll keep a good grip on your horse's reins."

Lynnet loved the timbre of his deep voice. Its sonorous masculinity sent shivers up and down her spine.

She strained to identify the voices of the other people arriving at the stables. She might just hear the voice of one of those men in the cellars or her kidnappers.

"It sounds like there are a lot of others traveling with us."

"Quite a few," Matilda said. "Since the new palace is still being refurbished, a great many of us have had to stay here in the old palace. Inconvenient, but what can we do?"

When Lynnet's horse arrived, Basil lifted her easily onto the sidesaddle. The flesh where his broad hands spanned her waist seared hotly like a branding iron.

How strange. I like it.

Fleur appeared breathless when she arrived at Maximilian's chamber door. He was provoked that she had the gall to come unannounced. His wife, Lady Rosamund, was getting dressed for tonight's dance in the back chamber. The last thing he wanted was to have his wife overhearing his business.

"What are you doing here?" he hissed as he drew Fleur inside and shut the door. "I don't want anyone to see you in my hallway."

"I have news."

Maximilian cringed.

"Keep your voice down. My wife and her maid are in the back chamber. I don't want them to overhear."

Fleur whispered.

"My news is important. I hurried to get here before you left."

She puffed out her chest as if to emphasize the importance of her information.

"Listen to this. The Sheriff of London is escorting Lady Lynnet to the dance tonight. Lord Geoff and Lady Matilda are going with them to Westminster Palace."

Maximilian's heart dropped into his stomach.

"Bah. What bad news. I'll have to tell the others." He cringed again. "And tell my wife we can't go to the dance after all."

"I bet that will go over well," Fleur said as she inched her way back out the door.

Maximilian's anger rose.

"Rosamund will do as I say. She's learned not to oppose me."

Chapter Seven

The journey through the moonless night profoundly affected Basil. Somewhere along the miles covered during the hour-long ride, he developed an intense, protective feeling towards the blind woman on the smooth-gaited horse.

The protectiveness was not because she was helpless. Just the opposite. Her willingness to face a cold, hour-long ride on the back of an unknown horse impressed Basil. There was always the chance of the horse stumbling into a darkened pothole, a possibility that would have had some sighted women clinging to the saddle in terror. Lynnet sat upright, dignified and balanced.

The lack of light tonight gave him some understanding of the world she lived in day-to-day. The torches of the king's retainers were not sufficient to cut through the gloom of a moonless night. The shadows of the riders elongated and diminished as the landscape changed, creating a weird, moving pattern.

No wonder Lynnet is accused of seeing ghostly images.

If my horse stumbles and I end up sprawled like a fool in the dirt, well so be it. I'm not going to miss this dance because I'm petrified of something that probably won't happen.

The sharp bite of winter night air slid under her garments, chilling her. It had taken all her willpower to remain in the saddle when nearby horses spooked at the chaos caused by dozens of riders setting off at the same time. Despite erratic noises, her horse stayed calm, its head hung low, and followed meekly at the sheriff's tug on the reins.

Basil must have gotten me the most mild-mannered horse in the king's stables.

The trip home would be a challenge. She would be tired.

Lynnet didn't join the conversational banter. Despite the bitter wind blowing off the Thames, the party was in a happy mood and laughter rippled out into the night air.

Since both palaces bordered the Thames, the roadway followed the river. Basil set a slow pace and Matilda and Geoff didn't complain. They rode behind her, which was a relief. If she fell off at least someone would notice right away.

Relief surged through Lynnet when she finally heard the riders halting and dismounting.

After asking permission, Basil slid his hands under her heavy cloak to get a better grip. She ignored the effect his fingers had on her waistline when he lifted her off the leather sidesaddle as if she had no weight at all. A little unsteady on her feet from pins and needles in her left leg, she clung to his broad shoulders until she could regain her balance.

Lynnet put a hand on Basil's arm for guidance, aware of the heavy wool enveloping the man. The wool was not of the quality worn by her father, but definitely serviceable.

As they joined Matilda and Geoff on the dirt pathway to Westminster Palace, surrounding animated chatter excited Lynnet's curiosity.

"Tell me everything that's happening. I don't want to miss a thing."

Basil grimaced. Fashions and architecture were not his forté. Bashing heads together was more to his liking. But if it would make the lady smile, he'd do his best.

"Many are dressed in velvet and fur."

Basil, himself, was dressed conservatively in black wool. The only relief from black was a wide, blue ribbon strung through a bronze Seal of Office around his neck and his weaponry. He would have to leave his broadsword in the cloak room before entering the Hall. He hoped the slender knife secreted in his knee-high, black leather boot would be overlooked by the king's guards. If he uncovered the conspirators tonight, he wanted an advantage over them.

"I wish I could see."

The plaintive tone in her voice tore at his heart.

"Your beauty rivals any of the women attending."

As he said it, he realized he meant it. At first, he only wanted to make her feel better, to remove that sad tone from her voice. In looking around, he decided it was true. She was the most beautiful woman there. Even the vivacious Matilda could not match Lynnet's serene beauty.

"That's kind of you."

Lynnet's touch was featherlight on his arm, but it seemed to be enough for her not to stumble. Matilda and Geoff walked farther ahead on the smooth, dirt path. The darkness was lit intermittently by torches shoved into the earth along the pathway from the stables to the massive front door.

"The king seems to have every torch and candle lit tonight," he said. "All the windows are aglow, and there are a great many windows."

With the Anglo-Saxon rebellion suppressed, there was no

need to make Westminster into a fortress.

"It's an ornate palace built only twenty years ago by the king's deceased brother, Rufus."

"I know. My tutor told me it's a sight to behold."

"Your tutor's correct. The Hall dominates in the center, with wings on either side ending in rounded turrets. The arched window over the entrance is three-stories high. It's flanked by towering spires." To Basil, it looked like a cathedral, not a residence.

"Are you two all right back there?" Matilda asked, glancing quickly over her shoulder.

"We're fine," Lynnet said.

Basil patted Lynnet's gloved hand where it lay on his forearm. He admired her courage.

Immediately he felt embarrassed.

I've done it again. Twice in one day. I crush hands, not pat them.

"All the king's servants are dressed in purple and gold," Basil was saying. "At the door, porters are stationed. Anyone questionable will be blocked from entering. The king must be protected."

The conspirators' words flashed into Lynnet's mind.

"Caution is definitely wisc."

She could feel Basil start up steps. At the same time she heard, "Be careful. Stairs. They're not high, but they're wide."

Lynnet tried to match his stride so that her foot wouldn't catch an edge and slip off. It was a challenge.

Basil gave their names to the porters and they followed Geoff and Matilda inside.

"We'll leave our cloaks in a room outside the Great Hall. Servants will keep an eye on them."

Lynnet had worn her expensive fox fur cloak with a hood and red, velvet lining tonight. She hoped Basil thought it complemented her complexion and hair. Evelyn had said it did.

"Is the cloak room on the left?"

She could almost hear his jaw drop.

"I don't know how you do it, but you're right."

She grinned.

"Many years of practice. Not to ignore the fact that I can see some shapes. People are heading in that direction."

Bursts of conversation ebbed and flowed as their party entered the Great Hall. Laughter echoed and guests called out to friends. Basil frowned.

I have no friends in this crowd, other than Geoff.

The nobility turned a cold shoulder to illegitimate sons, especially those with few possessions. Only fear of offending his powerful father kept them civil.

That's of no concern. I do as I want.

Basil made Lynnet comfortable on a bench away from the crowd and against the wall, thinking as he did so that she looked beautiful in green velvet. She hadn't wanted to walk around the huge chamber, claiming a need to rest on something not moving underneath her.

Geoff and Matilda brought them food and drink since Basil refused to leave Lynnet's side. He didn't want the conspirators to gain even a sliver of time to spirit her away.

They were sitting quietly, finishing eating, listening to the musicians, not even talking. Occasionally, he helped her with her food.

He was surprised he wasn't restless. Usually sitting quietly was an anathema to him, but with Lynnet it was peaceful.

Lynnet was exquisitely aware of Basil as she sat next to him. Her skin seemed afire and her stomach full of butterflies. Her heart stepped up its beat and her breath seemed only capable of short, quick bursts.

This has never happened to me before.

She wished she could see the expression on his face. She wondered if it held any of the same feelings.

This is exactly what I wished for.

But her parents would never approve.

"I know that song," Lynnet was saying. "I can dance it. Put us on the end of the line so I don't bump into other dancers."

Her face was alight with excitement. Her unseeing eyes glowed in the candlelight.

He took her tiny hand in his and placed his own on her slender waist. His fingers tingled.

Enthralled, Basil watched Lynnet turn in the correct direction for each change of the dance pattern. When she pulled her hand from his grasp to give it to another dance partner, he suddenly felt bereft. Not since a child, when his father tore him away from his mother, had he felt such a loss. Yet, here she was only inches away and coming back to him. Now, the world was back in balance.

He'd never experienced these feelings before. Could he be falling in love?

Impossible.

She's second cousin to a queen. Too far above me.

Chapter Eight

The conspirators lounged at their ease in Count Courbet's chamber while they listened to Fleur's report. She remained standing, not having been invited to sit.

"Best of all, when I returned an hour late with dried-out bread and cold porridge, I brought with me a pot of the most awful-smelling manure."

The count thought her facial expression evil, which suited him perfectly. This was not a task for a do-gooder.

"While pretending to straighten the linens, I put my small pot inside her clean chamber pot and took its lid off."

She grinned.

"It didn't take long for the lady to get sick. The smell was even giving me a fit."

Laughter rang out in the chamber.

"Anything that torments that Anglo-Saxon bitch suits me," André said.

Fleur preened and fluffed her dark hair before continuing her tale.

"She demanded my lover give her a new servant. Of course, he claimed there were none to be had."

"Good work," Maximilian said, clapping his hands and looking gleeful.

Fleur smirked. "She can barely stand me, but she's stuck with me."

"Keep it up," the count said, tossing a small bag of coins to her. "Add some ghost sounds. Make her believe what she heard last week was imagined."

"My pleasure," Fleur said. "That Saxon bitch is too high and mighty for my taste."

The count smiled grimly.

"Get her so mixed up she won't know what's real."

Lynnet was seated in the de la Werreiur chamber, a plate of cheeses and bread chunks at hand.

"This new servant drives me mad. She does everything wrong."

Even escorting her this morning, Fleur had gotten it wrong. She'd turned left, insisting it was the correct direction. Only Lynnet's refusal to budge convinced Fleur to turn right.

Who knows where we would have ended up!

She'd then tried to drag her too far down the corridor, but Lynnet had trailed her fingertips along the wall and counted the doors as they passed. She had dismissed Fleur as soon as Geoff opened the door.

Would it be possible to do without a servant for a few days? Just until Evelyn gets well. The thought nearly paralyzed her, but it might be better than all this aggravation.

"When they're new, you can't expect much," Matilda was saying.

"Especially now," Geoff added. "I'm sure the king's staff is stretched to the limit."

Lynnet touched the wooden plate until she found a good-sized piece of soft cheese. She took a bite and chewed with pleasure. *This is the first un-stale cheese I've had all day.*

"She swears she's not moving the furniture when she cleans. But she must be." Bewildered, Lynnet wagged her head. "I've bumped into more things these past two days than I did in the last two weeks. I hear things, but I can't be sure."

"She probably doesn't understand that even slightly out of place is significant," Matilda said.

She and Geoff were sitting on the edge of the bed, holding hands. Winter sunlight poured around them from the opened window. Lynnet could almost feel the love they had for each other.

Thoughts of Basil crept in and, with them, a momentary sadness for things not to be.

She forced her mind back to Fleur.

"She brings all the worst food. It's like she waits until everyone else gets the best pickings and then she chooses mine."

"You poor dear," Matilda said.

Lynnet wrung her hands.

"Rescue me. Walk me to the Hall for midday meal."

"My dear, we can't. We're eating with friends today in their chamber."

Lynnet's heart sank. She gritted her teeth and squared her shoulders.

"I'm desperate. I'll ask my parents."

"You really shouldn't lower yourself by being seen socially with that Norman," Lynnet's mother was saying as they walked to the Hall for midday meal. Passersby murmured greetings. Lynnet replied, but her parents ignored them. None was the voice of the men in the cellars.

"I heard all about your dancing with him last night." Her mother's voice took on an indignant tone as she sniffed, "He's a mere sheriff, with no lands of his own."

Lynnet turned to her father for aid, but got none. He soothingly patted her hand that rested on his forearm, but agreed with his wife.

"You really need to be more attentive to family dignity, Daughter."

"He's a friend of Lord Geoff's," Lynnet protested. "I was going to the dance with Lady Matilda and her husband. The sheriff offered to be my escort. He's educated and mannerly."

"That's another thing," her mother said, her voice dripping with disdain. "I can't understand why a highborn like de la Werreiur would lower himself to marry the daughter of a blacksmith." Lady Durwyn sniffed. "Even a Norman should know better."

"But they love each other," Lynnet insisted, her heart throbbing erratically from misery.

Her mother drew in a sharp breath. Her tone was icy.

"Love? What does that have to do with marriage?"

Chapter Nine

Basil broodingly paced his bedchamber, his hands clasped tightly behind his back, his upper torso slanted as if striving forward towards some objective.

Because of the king's commission, Basil ranked high on the chamberlain's list for a comfortably furnished chamber. A large, carved, four-poster bed with heavy, lined draping kept out the cold night air. Two leather-slung chairs and a carved walnut writing desk with its own high-backed chair were to the right of the door near the window.

This morning, Basil had the window shutters cracked opened to allow in fresh air. His assigned servant had started a roaring fire at dawn and the heat from the fireplace was still too much. He didn't like overheated rooms.

He was trying to piece together the puzzle his investigations had become. The inventory revealed that only those supplies hard to identify were being pilfered. Seeds, flours, spices and salt disappeared while armaments and furnishings were left alone. He was getting nowhere with the thefts.

The winter sun etched wavering patterns on the gray floor stones, echoing the framed panes of window glass. Basil had an irrational urge to hop and skip among the various shapes. Anything to lighten the burdens of this day.

Yesterday, he'd never told Lynnet he was investigating the

men in the cellar and her kidnapping. His first opportunity had been thwarted by Geoff. At the dance, he didn't want to crush her carefree mood.

He turned abruptly and strode towards the door. He would visit the lady.

"Maybe she'll remember something now she's had time to think."

Lynnet was braiding a rug. She sat in a comfortable chair near the fireplace working the sewn-together cloth strips into a snug braid, using a hooked, wooden tool.

Before Evelyn had gotten ill, the companion had cut the strips of usable cloth salvaged from old clothing and sewn them together into a long cloth tail of sufficient length for a small rug. Lynnet then wound these lengths into balls, which Evelyn sorted by color into different shaped baskets.

Lynnet cocked her head to one side. There it was again. She couldn't have imagined it.

"Who else is in the room?"

"Just us, my lady," Fleur said.

Lynnet was aware her hearing was better than most people's. Still, she thought these noises loud enough to be heard. She'd even picked out a word. It was "murder". Or perhaps "murmur".

"Are there people outside my door? I heard voices."

"Not that I can tell, my lady. But I'll go look."

Lynnet heard Fleur put down the candlestick she was polishing and cross the bedchamber to open the heavy door. "No one is out here."

She closed the door and re-crossed the room to the side table where she'd been working. As she passed Lynnet, she said, "Ghosts."

Lynnet's stomach tightened. No one mentioned ghosts around her. Her parents forbade it.

After losing her sight as a child, Lynnet was comforted by a ghostly figure of her paternal grandmother. Coming to her a few times a year, it usually got her out of dangerous situations. At eight years old, this seemed perfectly natural. She remembered her mother's fury the first time she spoke of it.

"Just like my mother-in-law to interfere with my business after she's dead."

She warned Lynnet not to mention this apparition again.

While Lynnet had heeded the advice of speaking to no one, she ignored the advice to shun the apparition. It had never spoken before. To do so now after a decade of silence seemed strange.

Lynnet rested the cloth braid on her lap and slowly twisted on her chair to study the chamber. Although she heard the low, gruff voice again, no apparition was present. She faced Fleur, who was still bent over her work at the side table.

"What did you say?"

"Nothing, my lady."

"I heard someone speak."

"I said nothing, my lady. The only time I speak is in answer to your questions."

Lynnet was incredulous. Her gut instinct said Fleur was lying. But to what purpose? The Tower's chamberlain had assigned her. They had never met before two days ago. It made no sense for Fleur to jeopardize her position.

"Maybe you're hearing ghosts," Fleur suggested. "They say the Tower has ghosts."

ꝏ

Basil knocked forcefully on Lady Lynnet's chamber door. It swung open shortly thereafter to reveal the same voluptuous, dark-haired maidservant with the mischievous air. In earlier days, her provocative ways would have captured his interest. These days, his interest was reluctantly captured by a flaxen-haired beauty.

"Please ask your mistress for a moment of her time."

"Come in, Sheriff," he heard Lynnet call out.

His armaments clanged as he entered. He felt awkward bringing weapons into a gentlewoman's chamber, but it was too late now. He should have thought of that before impulsively rushing here.

"Fleur, bring the sheriff a mug of ale. Then leave us. Return in an hour."

Lynnet looked extra pale, her face framed by an ecru-colored linen cap. She was wearing an ecru gown, giving the illusion of her fading into the grayness of the wall.

Whoever chose this unflattering color did not do her a service.

"Come sit with me, Sheriff," Lynnet said, indicating a stool across from her by the fireplace. She had some kind of colorful needlework spilling over her lap and into an unruly pile of cloth strips lodged in a wicker basket at her feet.

He accepted a wooden goblet from the servant who seemed reluctant to leave the chamber. Basil glared at the maidservant until she left, securely closing the door behind her.

"What brings you here, Sheriff?"

Basil was amazed how Lynnet used her other faculties to

make up for the loss of sight. She had waited until the exact moment when the maidservant could no longer overhear. He could well believe she heard a conversation a corridor away.

"To warn you to be careful."

"I've been extra careful lately," she assured him.

Basil swallowed some ale and gazed at Lynnet's pale face briefly before continuing. Memories of their dance last night drifted across his mind's eye.

"I'm investigating the conversation you overheard."

"I'm glad."

"My investigations lend validity to your testimony," he said, discomforted that he did not realize this straight away.

"I'm glad you now believe me."

"Have you remembered anything more since our earlier conversations?"

"I'm afraid not."

"Has anything out of the ordinary been happening?"

Lynnet fiddled agitatedly with the braided material on her lap.

"The only strange thing in my life is this new servant assigned to me since my companion got ill."

"What do you mean?"

"The chamberlain must have scraped the bottom of the barrel to find Fleur. I tried to get him to give me another, but he said there is none to be had."

This servant didn't look like a bottom-of-the-barrel choice.

I wonder what's going on here.

"She does everything wrong," Lynnet said as she twisted the cloth braid between her fingers. "She moves the furniture and brings me the worst food. She mutters in a low voice. I swear she sometimes sounds like a man. I only catch a word here and there."

Lynnet was getting increasingly upset. Basil decided this was worth pursuing.

"How does she explain herself?"

"She doesn't."

"What do you mean?"

"She tells me she hasn't said a word. She tells me I must be hearing the ghosts of men who died in the basement cells."

"I'm in charge of those cells. Believe me, there are no ghosts."

He watched Lynnet feel along the cloth strip until she got to the end of a braid. She picked up a wooden hook and continued with the braiding, attacking the cloth fiercely. Something about this new servant had driven Lynnet to desperation.

"Is your own servant getting better?"

"I don't know. The apothecary said to stay away. He says she needs a chance to recover."

"I'd visit her. Bad food should have passed through her by now."

"I will."

The small hairs on the back of his neck bristled. "But don't go alone."

"I won't. Matilda will come with me."

The timing of the companion's sickness deserved closer scrutiny. If he got right on it, he might have something for the king's deputy later today.

Basil rose to his feet. "I know a good woman. I'll see if she could help you until your companion gets well."

Lynnet looked instantly relieved.

"And I'll also have someone look into this new servant. Something's not right there."

"Bless you."

Chapter Ten

The dark, smelly, noisy room near the basement kitchens disheartened Lynnet. She had no idea servants were treated so badly in Norman castles.

I'll get Evelyn transferred to my bedchamber.

When she first arrived, Lynnet had remained rooted in the doorway, not knowing where to place her feet until Matilda brought a torch from the hallway. The one candle in the room did nothing to penetrate the murky darkness.

Her friend still stood in the doorway of the tiny chamber, well away from the two straw pallets covering most of the narrow floor. She was probably being cautious about getting bedbugs in her skirts. It was too late for Lynnet to fret about bedbugs. Without thinking and on hearing Evelyn's weakened voice, she'd knelt down beside her.

"I should have come sooner."

"You didn't know," Evelyn rasped. "You were warned away."

"That man must be incompetent. It shouldn't take four days for you to recover from bad food."

"I don't understand it myself. I can't seem to get better."

"There's no fresh air. No light. How can you be expected to heal in a room like this?"

Lynnet vowed to dismiss the apothecary.

"You should have told me when we first arrived that you had been allotted such an awful place. I would have demanded a chamber on an outer wall. At least there would be an opening for fresh air. And perhaps I could have gotten you one of your own."

The woman who shared this tiny hovel was at work in the kitchens. Lynnet could smell the stench of her unwashed clothing.

Evelyn wore several layers of clothing to keep warm because only one shabby, wool blanket protected her against the damp cold of the cellar. When Lynnet pulled it up over her companion, she had been shocked to feel how threadbare and coarse it was.

My parents may be disagreeable, but they'd never treat a servant this way.

"We are only here for two months," Evelyn rasped. "Soon we will be home."

Lynnet imagined a stiff breeze on her face and the lowing of cattle on her family's northern estate. These comforting barnyard sounds were precious to her. She wouldn't trade the countryside for all the riches of the king's court.

"You'll stay with me until you're well," Lynnet told Evelyn as she held her hand. "I'll get a trundle bed put into my chamber to get you off this cold floor. And I'm dismissing that incompetent apothecary. Matilda is a healer. She can watch over you."

"I'd be happy to," Matilda said.

Lynnet heard her friend place the torch into a wall sconce and step out into the corridor.

"I'll arrange with the chamberlain for the bed and find someone to carry Evelyn up the stairs. You stay here, Lynnet. I'll be back as soon as I can."

"I don't want to be a bother," Evelyn said.

Lynnet gave her companion's hand a squeeze.

"You're too dear to me to be a bother. Besides, you can help me keep an eye on that stupid servant they replaced you with. I swear the woman is worse than that apothecary."

Maximilian glared at Fleur. She had come unannounced to his chamber to declare she was not finishing her job.

"Return the money. You didn't get done what we asked."

Fleur jammed her hands onto her hips and stamped her foot. She glared back angrily.

"I would have if that devil's spawn hadn't dragged her sick servant into her bedchamber. You can't expect me to pull tricks in front of a sighted woman."

"There must be some way."

"There isn't. Besides, I've been dismissed. The sheriff is bringing in his own maidservant."

"Worse luck. Give back the money we paid you."

"Are you mad? I risked jail. Feel lucky I don't ask for more. I could spill my guts to the sheriff."

Maximilian's hands curled into fists at his side. Fury raged inside. Before he could decide what to do, Fleur fled the chamber, slamming the door shut with a vengeance.

His hands clasped behind his back and his head bowed in thought, he chewed his lower lip, concentrating.

Fleur had certain influence. She was mistress to the chamberlain, as well as accommodating several noblemen on occasion, including himself. From experience, Maximilian didn't trust her. If angered, she would delight in getting all of them jailed.

He straightened and threw his shoulders back.

He had to protect himself. Hide his possessions. This was every man for himself.

Maximilian strode forcefully across his bedroom and jerked open the door to his wife's compartment. She was sitting on a cushioned bench as her servant brushed her long, black hair.

"Get packed. We're leaving. Today."

Her mouth dropped open. "But...but..."

"And keep this quiet. I don't want anyone to know."

"You can't mean this. We have social obligations. The king will wonder."

"On second thought, be ready within the hour."

He returned to his chamber, slamming the door behind him.

Lynnet braided a small rug while her companion rested on a horse-hair mattress and clean bedding. Her probing fingers held the stretchy cloth loop wide so her right hand could push the wooden hook through the loop and grasp another section of cloth for a new loop before tightening the last one.

She was wearing a long-sleeved, high-necked, woolen kirtle, its train wrapped around her feet clad in felt-lined slippers to protect against chilling drafts seeping up from the floor. She'd been told a few snow flurries had fallen on and off the past two days, but the sun evidently held dominance today. Its rays lightened the shadowy patterns on the floor and warmed where it touched her cheeks. The screeching of a hawk on the hunt drifted through the unshuttered window.

Within easy reach was a small table with dried fruit and ale. She scooped some berries from the wooden bowl and tossed them into her mouth, savoring the release of their trapped sweetness.

Lynnet relaxed against the high back of a wooden chair nearby Evelyn's trundle bed, placed close to the fire for warmth. After a sound sleep and a hearty breakfast, Evelyn seemed considerably stronger and more like herself than she did yesterday.

Basil's servant had left a few minutes ago, carrying the dirty linen to the laundress.

Bless the man for getting that awful woman out of my life.

Thinking about him brought a secret smile to her lips.

Isolda had dressed Lynnet this morning without fuss, unlike Fleur who kept mixing everything up and insisting she had it right.

"I've noticed, Evelyn, I no longer hear strange voices since that woman left my service."

"I'm glad."

"I often thought she was talking to herself and not admitting to it."

Lynnet inserted the hook through the loop.

"And I'm feeling better," Evelyn said.

"What a blessing."

Feeling content for the first time in days, Lynnet leisurely braided the rug, occasionally humming.

Basil had ordered the informant, Nicolas, to meet with him in the anteroom of the Treasury. When he finished here, he would do another round of the cellar storerooms. Maybe he'd stumble across something, which would lead him to the thieves.

They sat at a sturdy wooden table, their backs to the closed door beyond which two armed guards stood sentry duty over the king's gold. Heads bent towards each other, they kept their voices low.

"Fleur," Nicolas was saying, "is the mistress of the chamberlain. He, in turn, seems friendly with Count Maximilian de Selsey, brother-in-law to Lord Geoffrey de la Werreiur. Count Maximilian is often in the company of your half-brother."

Basil frowned deeply.

"I know this Maximilian. He's a weasel."

Nicolas nodded his head in agreement.

"I don't know if the chamberlain is the third man or not. I'm fairly certain your half-brother and Maximilian are two of the men Lady Lynnet overheard. Your brother sounds like you and Maximilian speaks in a whiny voice."

Basil slammed a fist onto the table, making the mugs totter. Bile rose in his throat. He picked up a mug, squeezing tightly as if wringing his half-brother's neck.

"It will devastate our father."

Nicolas swallowed a deep slug of ale. He wiped his mouth with the back of his sleeve.

"Others from Chester stay here," he said. "The culprit could be a soldier garrisoned in the Tower."

"Doubtful. I've had enough quarrels with André to know his hatred of Saxons."

"What are you going to do?"

"I have to be absolutely sure. My father is fiercely loyal to the king. A legitimate son connected to treason will tear his heart out."

"I'll keep looking into this."

Basil swallowed the rest of his ale in big gulps as if hoping to eradicate the bad taste in his mouth.

"I hate to point this out," Nicolas said cautiously. "Your stepbrother is a hothead. That woman should watch out."

A cold chill traveled down Basil's spine. He had had his own experiences with that hot temper.

"And did you know Count Maximilian left hurriedly this morning."

"He what?"

"The Count ordered his horse saddled just after dawn. He left, taking his soldiers and leaving his wife behind. Lady Rosamund has been ordered to pack everything and return home immediately. She's upset. She doesn't want to leave the court."

"Gutless vermin! I'll get someone to follow him."

After Nicolas left, Basil rested his forehead on folded arms on the table. The solid wooden door was shut tightly so no one could intrude on this struggle of conscience. The burden of his responsibilities weighed heavily. He might have to arrest his father's legitimate son. Would he also be forced to jail his friend's brother-in-law?

Loyalty to fellow Normans had been hammered in from a young age by his father. He'd learned that lesson well. Loyalty now warred with his allegiance to justice. In the end, he must do what was right for the king, but his path would not be easy.

He dredged up memories of the first time he'd met his father, the Earl of Chester. His mother had always been silent on that score.

Basil's best friend in Ipswich, a raggedy 12-year-old who mostly lived on the streets, had been accused of stealing a rich man's coin purse. Although his friend had been with him at the time of the theft, the authorities would not listen and dragged his friend to jail.

The king had appointed the Earl of Chester to hear grievances when he traveled through Ipswich on his way to the court of France. When his friend was brought before the earl, Basil stepped out of the crowd and loudly affirmed that his friend could not be the thief because they were together at that time sweeping floors in the tavern.

After sending a soldier to verify the story with the landlord, the earl ordered Basil to come near him. He still remembered the fear that gripped him as he approached the flamboyantly wealthy and powerful earl.

"Who are you boy?"

"Basil of Ipswich."

"You have courage. How did you come by it?"

"My friend was falsely accused. I stand by my friends."

"As do I."

The earl leaned a little closer so the others in the hall could not hear.

"Who is your mother?"

"Jocelyn. Barmaid at the Golden Goose Tavern."

"I know her. How old are you?"

"Ten."

The earl massaged his chin as he spoke.

"I passed through Ipswich ten years ago."

The Earl of Chester's next words sealed Basil's fate, wrenching him from a mother's care and plunging him into a monastic life.

"By God, you're the spitting image of my eldest son as a child."

Chapter Eleven

Basil rode recklessly amongst pedestrians and horses and through flurried snow falling on deeply rutted, muddy roadways. His need to escape the confinement of the Tower drove him to take the longer river road where he could gallop his horse rather than the more direct route by city streets. Skill and determination alone carried him safely to his London quarters at the city jail.

He reined in his winded stallion so sharply its hooves slid on the wet paving stones. He threw the reins to the ragged boy in charge of rubbing down, watering and stabling horses at the quarters. Stepping over a high threshold, he walked rapidly towards a small room at the back. An experienced investigator from his London workforce would be arriving there soon. His man at arms greeted him and would have flooded him with questions except Basil put him off until after the meeting.

Basil's unease made the stifling air more bothersome than usual, even though the canvas window drape was drawn back to expose the stormy November day. The demands of the two investigations prevented him from getting out for his early morning rides. Amongst the forest trees, he could escape the stench from the river and the constant din of a castle teeming with people.

He shrugged his shoulders. "It can't be helped."

London is where his father found work for him. It would be the height of foolishness to turn his back on security to quench a longing for the countryside. If the investigations were successful, he'd ask for a select post outside of London. Patience was essential when dealing with the whims of those in authority.

I can wait and work for what I want.

Basil entered the meeting chamber, shut the door behind him, plopped into a chair and stretched his misused muscles. He braced his tired head on his hands, his elbows against his knees and rubbed his temples. He still had no answers for the thefts. Nor any hint where the stolen goods ended up.

Certainly not in the London marketplace. My spies found no evidence of that.

Apparently, the chamberlain was obeying the order to keep storerooms locked. One man kept an eye on him to determine if he was behind the thefts or even one of the conspirators. So far, he'd done nothing but carry out the duties of his office.

Even Fleur was keeping out of sight. Basil gritted his teeth, scowling.

I'll find that woman. Eventually. She'll pay for what she did.

Strangely, rage against Fleur evoked images of a serene Lynnet, stirring desire despite his worries. A heated itch caused Basil to shift uneasily on the wobbly chair. At the same time, a hopeless longing lodged itself in his heart, constricting his breathing.

"If only..."

A sharp rap forced his attention back to business. He opened the door to a burly man somewhat shorter than himself, but muscled from years of soldiering.

"Hail, Sheriff," Halévy said.

The sandy-haired man stepped into the small chamber and enveloped Basil in a bear hug.

"Cavorting with the Tower's rich and powerful seems to agree with you. Welcome back to the poor end of London."

Having been in the military together, they had remained friends over the years.

Basil dragged a chair to the scarred wooden table where a flagon of wine and platters of cheese and bread were laid out.

"Sit down. Let me dump my burdens on you."

The sandy-haired man laughed.

"Just what I need."

"It's confidential," Basil said as he took a seat. "A possible conspiracy against the crown."

"God's wounds."

Halévy sat down, poured some wine into a wooden goblet and drank as Basil described his investigations.

"Only this morning, the suspect left the Tower suddenly for his Wessex estates, leaving his wife behind to bring their baggage."

"Craven cur!"

Basil laid out Halévy's orders then added, "Report only to me. If anything happens to me, report to the king's deputy."

"Sounds grave."

The sheriff nodded in agreement.

"We're up against powerful men."

Halévy knew the countryside near Count Maximilian's lands. When dressed as an itinerant peddler, he'd easily blend in with the populace, whether town or country, making him valuable as a spy. An excellent tracker, he could also defend himself if a situation got ugly.

"If he tries to leave the country, bring him to me," Basil said. "In irons, if need be."

"It'll be done."

"If already gone, follow him to Normandy."

The man nodded.

"Otherwise, watch him. I want to know the people he meets and who sends him messages."

"Why don't I just clap him in irons and persuade him to talk?"

"Not until I'm sure about a plot against the crown. I need solid evidence. He has money and powerful friends." Basil ground his teeth. "It galls me to wait, but it's prudent."

The sheriff gave Halévy a leather pouch containing coins.

"There's enough for several changes of horses and transportation to Normandy, if need be. It's also enough to ensure the local sheriff's aid."

Halévy grunted acknowledgment and tucked the pouch inside his tunic without opening it.

"The count has a head start. You'll need to ride hard. Wear the king's colors and use this authorization to secure fast horses." Basil handed Halévy a parchment delineating his authority.

"You can rely on me."

"That's all, except become a peddler when near Wessex. We don't want the count to know of the king's interest."

Halévy got to his feet. He shoved a few chunks of cheese and an end of bread into his pocket.

"I'll take two pages with me to courier messages. They'll be kept in the dark about the mission."

The two men clasped hands.

"Hire as many men as you need."

"You'll get daily reports."

Later that afternoon, as Lynnet opened her chamber door, she put a finger to her lips. "Shhhh. Evelyn's sleeping."

"Why are you answering the door yourself?" a deep voice demanded.

She jerked, surprised. Instead of the expected maidservant laden with food, it was the sheriff whose voice declared bad humor. Unbalanced, she tumbled backward. Before she could fall, Basil had her in his arms, pulling her against a muscled body encased in leather. Her heart speeded up.

"I-I," she stammered, feeling foolish. "I thought you were the woman you hired to help me."

Before she got another sound out, his mouth clamped tightly onto hers and explored hers in a kiss. Heat built deep in her loins and she found herself rising on tiptoes to run her fingers along his beard. Teasing masculine scents blended with those of horse and leather.

Lynnet used to think she'd need instruction before her first kiss. In truth, no experience was needed. She released a sigh and pushed herself against him.

Basil's short-cropped beard pricked her chin as his mustache nestled against her upper lip. Warmth built. Shivers raced down her sensitized spine and into her curling toes. Sheer wonderment threatened to overwhelm her. Her tongue crept out seeking his.

Lynnet assumed Evelyn was still asleep. If not, she was making a good pretense of it.

As fast as it happened, so quickly was she thrust away. She struggled to bring order to her disordered emotions.

"Forgive me," Basil said in hushed undertones, his breathing erratic. "Fear for your welfare blinded my judgment."

"Do not overly chastise yourself," she whispered, her emotions a jumble.

Hearing Basil move farther into the room, Lynnet closed the door behind him and barred it. As she reached out to find the high-backed, wooden chair placed to the left of the door, her hand trembled. She heard the scraping of a chair pulled away from the table and saw his shadowed form folding down onto it. He spoke quietly, as if now mindful of her sick companion.

"I came to talk about your last servant."

"I would just as soon forget her."

She was feeling the loss of his lips and didn't want the detraction of an incompetent servant.

"I've discovered Fleur is mistress to the chamberlain."

Lynnet shook her head in disgust.

"So that's why he wouldn't cooperate. He didn't want his mistress to lose her position."

"It may be worse than that," Basil said. "She may have been hired to spy on you."

A cold chill ran down Lynnet's spine.

"Those voices making me think I was going mad were deliberate?"

"I have no proof, but I believe so."

"Why?"

"My guess is it was strictly for money. We believe she was working for one of the men you overheard in the cellars."

Lynnet's stomach knotted. Throbbing built behind her brow.

"Was Evelyn's sickness deliberate?"

"It's possible."

Sadness weighed down her heart. Evelyn came near death because of knowing her. Lynnet glanced to the trundle bed where she could barely make out the form of her companion.

"A woeful affair."

Basil moved on the chair as if he was reaching for something. She heard him chewing, probably on one of the pork rinds left out since last night.

"I'll have someone check on the apothecary," he said.

"Have you questioned Fleur?"

"She went into hiding after being released from your service."

"Unfortunate."

"Be extra careful from now on. Ask who it is before you open the door. If Fleur and the chamberlain and, maybe, the apothecary are corrupted, you can't trust any stranger."

Discomfited remembering what happened after opening the door and what might have happened, Lynnet changed the topic before the heated blush working its way up from her bosom became obvious.

"Are you making progress on learning the names of the men?"

"I may know two of them, possibly three. Until I have more than suspicion, I need to keep them confidential."

He wasn't dragging his feet. I should've had more faith.

She needed to make amends, if only to salve her own conscience for her lack of faith.

Basil rose and walked towards the door. Lynnet rose.

"I'd like to stay until Isolda arrives," he said, "but I cannot. I have work to do."

"Perhaps this evening you could stop by."

"If I get free, I will."

Her parents would be furious, but she wanted a chance to atone, as well as to explore the emotions aroused by Basil.

A slight frown creased her forehead.

And learn why he cut them off so abruptly.

Embarrassed, Basil gladly escaped Lynnet's chamber. Although she hadn't condemned him with words, he felt condemned by her restraint. And, yet, she'd responded to his kiss.

Recalling her tongue seeking entrance warmed him and stirred his manhood. Her vulnerability was his downfall. Exposing herself so completely by opening the door brought an anger, which overrode judgment and transformed into desire. His heart beat faster while remembering her body pressed against his. An upwelling of happiness surged through him as he approached Lord Geoff's door.

On the ride back from London headquarters, Basil had reached the conclusion that his friend could not be involved in conspiracy with his brother-in-law. A man so in love with a Saxon woman wouldn't be out to destroy them. Armed with that belief, he walked the remaining few steps to Lord Geoff's chamber door and knocked loudly.

"What a surprise," Geoff greeted him. "Come in."

"Is your wife here?"

"She's out visiting."

"Good."

Basil entered the chamber and collapsed into a chair at the table, scowling at his friend.

"I have something serious to discuss."

"Has something happened to Lynnet?"

"It's not Lady Lynnet. It has to do with your brother-in-law."

Geoff slammed his fist into the wall.

"What's he done now, the sadistic son of a whore? Is he lighting stray cats on fire?"

"I believe he's part of the conspiracy."

Geoff's face paled.

"He's one of the men Lynnet overheard?"

"I believe so."

Geoff sank into a chair, leaned his elbows on the table and ran his fingers through his thick hair. When he spoke, his voice sounded strained.

"He's always so conscious of family standing. His betrayal puts us all in jeopardy."

He looked up at Basil.

"How could he do this?"

"Out of hatred for Saxons."

Geoff stood and started pacing.

"That I can believe. He perverted my sister from a loving girl into a bitter woman. Now, my only sibling and I are estranged."

"So I heard."

"It's been difficult for me having married the daughter of an Anglo-Saxon commoner. Only my wealth and the king's protection keep the wolves at bay."

"It must strain your marriage."

"It would if we'd let it. We're so happy together we ignore those not happy for us."

Geoff stopped pacing and turned to Basil.

"What will you do to my brother-in-law?"

Basil rose.

"I can't discuss this further. Since you're my friend, I wanted to warn you what's coming down the pike."

Geoff clapped him on the back. "I appreciate that."

"Keep this confidential, even from Matilda."

"I will."

As Basil walked towards the door, he added, "Your brother-in-law left the Tower hurriedly this morning."

"He did?"

"He's on his way to Wessex. He could've gotten wind of my suspicions."

"The coward. He'll probably take his frustration out on my sister."

"Lady Rosamund is still at the Tower, packing."

"I'll try to get her to stay." Geoff sounded encouraged. "Let Maximilian stew in his own juices."

"Give me any intelligence on him you glean from her. Swear her to secrecy."

"I'll see what I can find out." Geoff's face looked strained. "I must keep my family clear of his doings."

Basil put his hand on the latch, but Geoff stopped him from opening the door.

"What are you going to do with Maximilian?"

"His destiny is in his own hands."

Chapter Twelve

"Maximilian flew the coop." Count Courbet de Shereborne squeezed the neck of his goblet so hard it felt like he would crush the wood by his bare hand.

"The yellow-bellied swine," Sir André de Chester said, noticeably agitated.

They were in Courbet's chambers. It was just before midday meal and they had taken great pains not to be seen together.

"Did he hold his tongue before fleeing?" André asked as he picked up a piece of cheese to eat.

"He sent us no message."

"We must assume the worst."

Courbet took a deep swallow of mulled wine.

"I sent a man after him. My man will slit his throat."

André nodded, accepting the judgment.

"It'll look like he died during a scuffle with thugs. The sheriff won't be able to connect us to his killing."

André scoffed. "My bastard brother can't touch us. We're too powerful."

"He can if the king is involved. King Henry wrested the throne from his elder brothers, imprisoning Robert. He'd crush us without a second thought."

André wiped nervous sweat from his forehead with the back of his sleeve. "We've been careful."

"Henry will throw us in irons if he even suspects. Plotting against the crown is treason."

André's handsome face turned ashen.

"But we're not," he protested. "We're just putting those damned Anglo-Saxons back in their place."

"Only because we've had no commitment from his imprisoned brother. Chicken-livered Robert refused to consider rebelling against his brother."

"And what about the stolen goods?" Courbet continued, forcing André to face facts. "Henry won't take kindly to those thefts."

"Money ranks high with Henry. If we pay him back threefold, all will be forgiven."

Courbet's stomach clenched. The man was whistling in the wind.

"Maybe. But this year it was too cold to get a good harvest. He may take the theft of grain as an affront to the crown."

André's voice was strained. "Don't overreact. We'll point suspicion at ourselves for sure if we do."

"We need to find out who knows what."

André ran his fingers underneath his collar as if it were getting hot under there.

"I have a paid spy in the king's staff. I'll get in touch with him to see what he's heard."

"Do that. If the king and the sheriff have gotten together, our situation is more desperate."

"We must silence our enemies so there's no one to testify against us."

"Like that blind woman from the cellars," Courbet said. "I understand she has exceptional hearing. One chance encounter where she identifies our voices will be our undoing."

"We can make her disappear."

"We can't afford another foul up," Courbet said, as he fingered the design carved into the goblet.

"The men were getting a boat," André protested. "They never expected her to wake up."

"We need something more permanent."

André stretched his long legs and crossed them at the ankles. He leaned back in his chair, folding his hands behind his neck to cushion his head.

"I'll come up with an idea that'll make her death look accidental."

Courbet sank down into his chair, deciding today would be a good day to get roaring drunk.

As soon as Basil left, Geoff wasted no time getting to his sister's chamber in the other wing of the castle. The door was flung open and Rosamund was instructing two maidservants in the packing. She turned when she heard his footsteps and glared at him, hands on hips.

"Well, Brother, did you come to gloat? My husband has left me stranded."

"Tell them to leave. We must talk."

"When you took Matilda's word over mine last summer, you destroyed any chance for us to talk."

"Listen to me now or you may have no future. Dismiss your servants."

A frown creased Rosamund's smooth, ivory skin. She brushed a stray lock of ebony-colored hair from her forehead with the back of a slender hand before turning to the servants.

"Get out."

The two women scurried out. Geoff stepped into the chamber, closing the door firmly behind him, looking around.

His sister lived in style. Her bedding was mostly silks and furs. The clothing laid out about the room was of the finest wool, many fur-trimmed. The raised lid of her jewelry coffer revealed precious stones. She didn't offer him a chair. He took one anyway, turning the oak chair backwards and sitting with his hands grasping its high back.

Rosamund sat primly on the edge of her bed since her clothing was strewn over the other chairs.

"Well, what is it?"

"Is there anyone in that other chamber?" he asked, pointing to an open door.

"You chased everyone away."

Now that he was here, Geoff was having a hard time getting started. He was unsure how much his sister knew about her husband's affairs. He wet his lips with his tongue.

"We've not been on the best of terms of late. Maximilian started the estrangement between us."

Rosamund looked disgusted.

"You came here to rake through old ashes?"

She got up and started pacing, waving her arms in agitation.

"What do you know about my husband? You avoided the two of us as much as possible since my marriage."

Geoff winced at her ferocity.

"You married for money," he said. "You should've been more discriminating."

"I have all this."

The vibrant blue of her long sleeve shimmered in the rays of the winter sun coming through the window as she gestured towards her possessions.

"He may drag you down with him."

"What are you talking about?"

"I don't want you arrested as his accomplice."

"Arrested?" She looked horrified. "Accomplice to what?"

"I need to know Maximilian's movements these past months."

"You want me to inform on my husband?" Her jaw dropped as if astounded. "I'm a loyal wife."

"You may know something that could clear him of suspicion."

"Suspicion of what?"

It was obvious that Maximilian didn't let Rosamund in on his dealings. Still, Geoff needed something to give Basil to show that his family was loyal.

"I cannot give particulars. I'm under oath. I can only say that Maximilian has been up to things that may end in the loss of his head."

"What?" she screeched.

"We believe that's why he left so hurriedly today."

All the color drained from his sister's face. Rosamund sank onto the bed and leaned her head against the bedpost.

"Why? Why would you warn me? I almost killed Matilda."

He could feel her despair.

"Because you're family. I protect my family. You weren't thinking clearly when you put Matilda in danger."

Rosamund ran a hand across her brow.

"What shall I do?"

"I'll take you to the sheriff. Answer his questions. He must be the one to tell you what Maximilian's done."

That afternoon, Matilda visited Lynnet. Geoff had gone off to a meeting with Basil and she felt in need of company. They were talking quietly while Evelyn dozed. Lynnet's pale hair had been left loose to flow about her face. Matilda was struck by her fragile beauty.

"At first, Basil scared me," Lynnet was saying as she fidgeted with the wool cuff of her burgundy gown. "He's so different from my scholarly father."

Matilda didn't know where this conversation was going. She reached across the table to select a sweetmeat. As she put it into her mouth, she decided not to commit herself until she understood what Lynnet wanted her to say.

"Understandable."

Matilda patiently watched dust motes drift through the sunlight filtering through a partially opened shutter. Eventually, Lynnet picked up the threads of her conversation.

"He needs to protect those he thinks weaker than himself."

"Admirable."

"He thinks I'm weaker because of my sight."

"Men don't always understand that strength goes beyond brawn."

Lynnet reached out to the table to judge where to set down her cup of cider.

"He's quite intelligent. He was educated by monks."

"I should've known that," Matilda said. "Basil's too well spoken for a tavern brat."

Lynnet flushed. Matilda had a hard time hearing her next words, so quietly were they spoken.

"I'm developing an affection for him."

Matilda's breath stopped. She suspected it, but never expected her friend to admit to it.

"My parents warn me against Normans."

Matilda's blood heated up.

"Geoff's Norman."

"I meant no offense." Lynnet seemed agitated, as if she were arguing with herself.

"Basil's illegitimate."

"I admire a man who rises above humble beginnings. Besides, his father is a powerful earl who claims him for his own."

Lynnet could do worse than choose Basil.

"It's not to say that marriage between a Saxon and a Norman isn't difficult," Matilda continued. "Despite Geoff's prominence, I get cold shouldered. Especially by my arrogant sister-in-law, as you heard in the Hall. Remember, I'm the daughter of a blacksmith, even though my mother's related to an earl."

"My parents don't think Basil's suitable."

This is the crux of the problem. Only a husband they chose would be suitable.

She worried for her friend. Whether she defied her parents or not, Lynnet's heart could end up broken. Matilda jumped up and started pacing.

"Geoff took a chance. He upset folks by marrying me, but we're happy."

Lynnet looked encouraged.

"Besides, no Saxon noblewoman can be forced into marriage."

"If angered, my parents could shut me away in a nunnery."

"I risked all and found love. It could've gone the other way. I almost died."

Her heart thumped erratically at the memory. She stopped in front of Lynnet and grasped both her hands tightly.

"In the end, you must decide how much to risk to take."

Chapter Thirteen

Despite the churned, watery slush underfoot, Lynnet gladly strolled across the Tower courtyard with Basil. The slush was probably ruining her expensive boots, but she didn't care. She hadn't been outdoors since the dance last week.

The cold air smelled like more snow was imminent. She pulled the fur-lined hood of her wool cloak tighter around her ears and neck. Both hands were hidden in a fur muff.

The moonless night created darkness so deep she could only see shapes when passing a wind-whipped torch. Her arm wove through Basil's, deliberately trapping him close. She leaned her head against his wool-clad arm, using it to determine when he changed directions. The hilt of his dagger pressed into her wrist where her hand entered the muff.

This was her world, a world of touch and smell and taste.

A sighted woman might have found such a dark and unsettled night unsavory. Not Lynnet. The bite of the wind on her cheeks, the brush of Basil's thigh, his rich voice dominating even the echoing calls of the night guards brought joy.

Basil's only spoken words were intended to keep her from stumbling over obstructions. She wondered if his emotions churned like hers, whether, still embarrassed by this afternoon's kiss, he could dredge up no social banter.

It doesn't matter. I prefer this quiet time.

She breathed deeply, pulling the chilled air inside herself, melding it with her body's warmth. The night watchman called out the hour. It was but three hours 'til midnight.

Perhaps an illusion, but Lynnet swore she heard Basil's heart beating through his heavy, wool cloak. Its rhythmic cadence soothed her. Her own eager heart sought a matching rhythm.

"I take pleasure in your company," she said.

Basil stumbled, but he quickly regained control.

"And I in yours."

The ghostly image of her benevolent grandmother appeared in a corner of the courtyard, seeming to nod her head in approval.

Lynnet smiled, content.

A half-hour after Basil returned Lady Lynnet safely to her servant, the informant, Nicolas, arrived in the Treasury Room of the Tower. Basil was anxious for news. He had to report tonight to the king's deputy.

"Your brother sells more grain than his land produces," Nicolas said after settling himself at the table.

"Do you think he's connected with the thefts as well as the conspiracy?"

"Seems that way."

So the thieves are also the conspirators.

Discouraged, Basil shook his head. There was no way he could keep his family name out of this mess. His brother would, at the least, be charged with theft.

He dismissed Nicolas with new instructions and started composing his report in his head.

How could André be so foolish!

Shortly before midnight, Basil was sequestered in his chamber with the king's deputy who was comfortably seated in a leather-slung chair with a goblet of wine in his hand. Logs had recently been added to the fire. They crackled, burning brightly, providing most of the light in the chamber. Basil twirled the stem of his empty goblet absentmindedly as he tried to pull the words of his report from his head. Thoughts of Lady Lynnet interfered. She seemed to be reaching out to him tonight.

The deputy cleared his throat and Basil refocused.

"The thieves have been lying low. There have been no thefts since I padlocked the storerooms."

"Good news.

"Highway robberies decreased since winter court began. That indicates the leaders are in attendance at court."

"Hmmm."

"As far as we can determine, all are Normans. No Anglo-Saxons are involved."

Lord Otheur nodded. "That's what the king suspected."

Basil swallowed and moistened his lips with his tongue.

"Just tonight I found a connection between the robberies and the conspirators."

"Excellent."

Mounting unease caused his throat to constrict. Beads of sweat linked more closely with anxiety than the blazing fire broke out on Basil's forehead.

"Loath as I am to admit this, my half-brother appears involved in both the thefts and the conspiracy. I'm told André sells more grain than his lands produce. His voice was the one in the cellars sounding like mine."

The deputy looked stormy.

"The king cannot turn a blind eye."

"I know that."

"He must be punished if involved."

"That's only just."

Basil swallowed to wet his throat. He poured some wine for himself and continued.

"My brother is being watched. We believe Count Maximilian de Selsey is involved as well."

Lord Otheur slapped his hand hard against the tabletop. Some wine from Basil's newly filled goblet splashed on the table.

"King Henry is already angry with him for leaving court without permission," the deputy said. "This will be his downfall."

"He probably suspected I was investigating and left while his hide was still intact."

"Better to have him wary than causing havoc."

"Not necessarily. If they do nothing, I get nothing."

"I see," the deputy said, drinking some wine.

"I sent a man after the count. If Maximilian tries to escape to France, he'll be taken into custody."

"What about the third man?"

Basil traced the carving on his wine goblet with his thumb. He wished he had better news.

"Still unknown."

"Unfortunate."

"For awhile I thought it was the chamberlain, but I've changed my mind. I believe the third man is more powerful than a chamberlain."

"Seems logical."

"According to my spies, my half-brother carouses in the Hall with any number of nobles. In his room, André has no visitors except women."

"No help on that score."

"So far we've uncovered no physical threat to the king. The trouble is directed against Anglo-Saxons. But continue to keep the king well guarded."

"I will."

Basil leaned across the table.

"I want to draw the unknown man into the open."

"How?"

"I'm accompanying the woman who overheard the plot to tomorrow's banquet. I'll make sure we're seen together. I'd like you to arrange with the king to spend time with Lady Lynnet and me. The conspirators will assume she told me about them and consider me a threat because I have the king's ear."

The deputy looked at Basil, thoughtfully.

"Risky. Especially for the lady."

"She's protected by friends, as well as by me. I've assigned a man to keep an eye on her."

"What about your safety?"

"I'll make a point of being alone. Only, I won't be. My men will be watching."

Lord Otheur nodded, then rose, ending the meeting.

"You have the king's gratitude. I'll make arrangements for tomorrow night."

Before opening the door, the deputy turned to Basil.

"Be careful. It's a dangerous game you play."

Chapter Fourteen

Lynnet spoke to her parents in their chambers. She'd waited impatiently until their servants removed the remnants of the morning meal and left, closing the door behind themselves.

"The sheriff is escorting me to the banquet tonight."

"You shouldn't be seen with him."

She could hear the distaste in her mother's voice.

"He's a Norman," her father added, as if that alone was enough to condemn him.

A chill entered the chamber as a gust of winter air blew through the opened window.

This would be a good time for my ghostly grandmother to appear and give a nod of approval.

Lynnet stiffened her backbone. "He's the acknowledged son of an earl. He studied at a monastery and holds the confidence of the king. Surely, that's enough to give the man some merit."

"He has no wealth."

"His offer is one of protection. He feels I could be harmed in a large crowd."

"I suppose I can tolerate him if my friends know he's there in his capacity as sheriff."

The haughtiness irked Lynnet. She wished her mother would concentrate on Basil's admirable qualities instead of his social inequality.

"You and father will be busy with your friends."

"That's true."

"The sheriff wants to make sure I'm not left on my own and spirited off again."

"I should have realized," her mother said, "there was nothing personal in his offer. Considering your blindness."

"Let him carry out his duty," her father added. He appeared to be brushing crumbs off his clothing.

Lynnet's heart shriveled, squeezing the joy out of her anticipation.

Although still weak, Evelyn almost felt her old self. She yearned to dress Lynnet for tonight's banquet, but both her mistress and Isolda would not hear of it. Sitting on a high-backed chair near the warmth of the crackling fire, she kept a motherly eye on things.

Isolda was brushing Lynnet's waist-long hair with more vigor than finesse, but the result was satisfying. The pale strands came alive and glowed from the oil worked into them. The servant's plump hands divided the thin, straight hair into sections and braided them together with a brilliant-blue ribbon.

Realizing Lynnet did not normally weave ribbons into her hair, Evelyn asked, "Who are you planning to impress?"

"No one."

"Tell me about this sheriff of yours."

"Nothing to tell."

After wrapping the braid around Lynnet's head, Isolda pinned it in place and added a small veil.

Lynnet followed her to the opened chest. Evelyn sat,

bemused, as the two women debated various pieces of clothing. A dark-colored, long-sleeved, high-necked velvet was the final choice.

"You seem to be making a lot of fuss," Evelyn said as she watched Lynnet reject another brooch.

Isolda held up a golden one. "What about this one? It's gold with five petals and a red stone in the middle."

"Perfect!"

"Velvet and gold?" Evelyn said. "This man must be special."

Lynnet wrinkled her nose at her companion. "Special? No. I'm just excited about getting out into society. I've been trapped in this chamber most of the week."

Knowing Lynnet's penchant for the quiet life, Evelyn laughed. "Tell that to someone who doesn't know you as well as I do."

"The sheriff is just doing his duty. Protecting me."

"Of course, he is."

"I've cleaned and cooked for him since he became sheriff," Isolda said in his defense. "An honorable man."

"I'll admit he has a captivating voice," Lynnet said.

"Does it make shivers run up and down your spine?"

"Of fear, maybe," she protested.

A blush started at Lynnet's neck and worked its way up to her face. Evelyn decided that more than fear caused those shivers.

Lynnet stepped into the midnight-blue gown with Isolda's help, settling it over shoulders and hips. The maidservant started tying the fasteners.

"Before we leave London, I'm going to set eyes on this intriguing sheriff. I'm always asleep when he calls."

Lynnet shoved her hands on her hips and stamped a leather-clad foot.

"When he comes tonight, don't you dare tease."

"My, my, aren't we being touchy."

Basil impatiently waited while the guests who arrived in the Great Hall before him and Lady Lynnet were presented to the king and his daughter. At last, their turn came.

"Basil of Ipswich, Sheriff of London, and Lady Lynnet, daughter of Lord Wilfgive of Osfrith and Lady Durwyn," the Master of Ceremony announced to King Henry, Lady Maud and his honored guests seated on the dais.

Tonight was a formal affair. The guests were emissaries from the French court. Only the titled were in attendance in the Hall. Others were being fed in the kitchens. Dogs had been rounded up and shooed out, flagstones swept, and new rushes laid. Musicians played.

Instead of moving them on immediately after being announced as he did with other guests, King Henry leaned forward and took one of Lynnet's hands in a fatherly gesture.

"Now here's a charming woman we haven't seen for a few days. Where are you keeping yourself?"

Lynnet curtsied.

"My companion was ill. I've been nursing her back to health."

"Be careful of your own health. We don't want anything happening to you."

"I'm being well cared for, Your Highness."

"Visit me sometime, Cousin," his daughter said, leaning forward in her chair to briefly clasp Lynnet's hand just released by her father. "We had no chance to chat at the dance."

"I will."

"Are your parents with you?"

Lynnet turned her head as if she could see. "They're supposed to be here. They came separately."

The king turned to Basil.

"Well, Sheriff, are you attending to the king's business?"

"Remaining diligent, Your Highness."

"We're counting on you. You're the man we depend on to keep the peace."

"I'm honored to have your support," Basil said loud enough for those around him to hear.

There. I hope that starts them worrying.

Just as the king signaled for the next guests to move forward, the king's daughter intervened. She made a comment that started Basil's heart pounding.

"What a good-looking couple you two make," Lady Maud said. "One golden, the other dark."

Chapter Fifteen

The next morning, Courbet and André rode separately into the king's forest, meeting under a bare-limbed elm. They remained astride their mounts in order to leave hastily if anyone happened by.

A feeble sun peered out from behind grayed, drifting clouds, barely softening patches of frozen snow. Puffs of steam rose from their breaths as they blew on cold hands. The early-morning air had a bite to it.

"They both have to die," André said as he ruthlessly controlled his restless mount. "They have the ear of the king. They're too dangerous."

"We don't know that. Neither of us was close enough to hear."

"They were given considerably more time than others."

"It looked more like family talk. You saw how Lady Maud joined in. After all, the woman is related."

"I don't like it."

"Well, neither do I."

They sat, silent, for a few minutes while each thought about the predicament. Any action they took could not draw attention to themselves.

"What about your man on the king's staff?"

"He's seen no documents. Heard nothing. If they're investigating us, they're playing it close to the chest."

Courbet circled his mount slowly around while he thought, intending to keep the horse warmed up against the cold.

"That sniveling coward Maximilian left us holding the bag," André complained.

Irritated, he jabbed a spur into his horse, causing it to rear. Its hooves slipped on the icy ground. André fought to bring it under control.

"It may be just as well Maximilian's gone. You and I don't wilt under pressure."

"He'll get his own soon enough."

"I believe the king knows nothing," Courbet said. "Otherwise, we'd be imprisoned."

"We must silence those two before Henry finds out."

"Anything we do has to look like an accident."

André smirked. "I can invite my brother hunting. You can put an arrow through him."

Courbet shook his head.

"He'd never go. The only thing you two do together is fight."

"Then I'll provoke a fight this evening when it's too dark to see clearly. I'll have my man sneak out and stick a knife into him."

"How will you explain a knife during a fistfight?"

"A disgruntled felon he once arrested. I'll say I heard a yell about revenge."

Courbet nodded his head.

"That takes care of your brother. What about the lady?"

"She always has people around her. That makes things more difficult."

Courbet pulled up his mount. "Whatever happens to her needs to be close to your brother's death. Otherwise, when she hears about it, she may start crying 'foul play'."

"Agreed. We can't chance people believing her."

"I'll see she disappears once and for all tonight."

André set up the ruse of being progressively drunker as the evening wore on. He made himself obnoxious to those nearby, upsetting everyone enough for his brother to intervene. Although Lady Maud and the king left the chamber almost an hour earlier, the French guests were still at the table. André caught scowls directed his way.

Perfect. Complain to the sheriff and get me thrown out.

He started singing loudly, out of tune, slurring the words of a bawdy song, embarrassing the women. From the corner of his eye, he saw his brother approaching and was not surprised when a hand clamped onto his shoulder.

"Settle down. You're disturbing the king's guests."

André deliberately turned slowly on his stool. He looked up at his brother, hoping he looked bleary-eyed.

"Well, if it isn't Big Brother."

"Get yourself to bed. You're making a nuisance of yourself."

André knocked the hand off his shoulder.

"Let me be."

"You need to leave."

"Get away from me."

André pretended to take another long drink of wine, deliberately allowing the goblet to tip over when he faked setting it down. Red wine scattered in all directions across the wooden table, making people jump out of the way to keep their clothes from getting splattered.

"That's it."

A powerful hand grasped the back of his collar and hauled him up into the air. His stool crashed backwards onto the flagstones.

I'll need to keep my wits about me. My brother is a strong son of a bitch.

André struggled in earnest, making sure his struggles were believable, but not so much that his brother called for the guards. The fate he planned for Basil depended on their being alone.

André allowed himself to be dragged kicking and protesting across the Hall. He was relieved when Basil turned left, heading towards the bedchambers, instead of handing him over to the guards at the door.

"You can't bully me with your wharf-rat tricks."

He deliberately slurred the words. André hoped he sounded so drunk Basil would believe he could not carry out threats. Surprise was an important element. "I'll get you for this."

"Shut up," Basil said. "People are trying to sleep."

Despite his dragging his feet, Basil had gotten him all the way to his chamber corridor. André gloated. The assassin was hiding in the shadows two-thirds of the way down.

"I always hated you."

"The feeling is mutual," Basil said.

A shiver went through André. The edge to Basil's voice sounded as if his brother had already put out coin to buy him a winding sheet.

Well, the feeling is indeed mutual.

"Our father was a fool to acknowledge you."

"Perhaps he saw in me the honor missing in you."

Anger surged through André. He swept his leg out, catching Basil sharply on the side of the knee, making him lose his grip and stumble.

Basil's grunt of pain awoke André to his mistake. He should've waited until they were farther down the corridor, closer to the assassin. Temper goaded him into premature action.

Too late now. I need to take the advantage.

Before Basil could recover, André struck him. The blow hit true, snapping Basil's head back with a satisfying crack. André cocked his right hand and swung again, but Basil turned so it slid harmlessly by.

André found it hard to pretend drunkenness and still fight his brother. He did his best to rain curses and blows. When Basil fell down from a second kick to the injured knee, André pretended to stumble drunkenly down the corridor towards his bedchamber.

"See. I'm better than you," he called over his shoulder.

From the corner of his eye, he saw Basil push himself to his feet and limp after him. When he spotted the assassin in the shadows, André pretended to fall down drunk to the flagstones. Basil limped up and leaned over him.

"You're more trouble than you're worth, Little Brother."

The assassin sprang, his knife arched down to stab Basil between the shoulder blades.

"Die, Sheriff. Feel my revenge for false imprisonment."

The assassin's words, meant to turn suspicion away from André should any guests overhear, warned Basil. He turned to deflect the knife, receiving a slanting cut across his back and upper arm through the layers of clothing.

André yanked his brother's arm, pulling him off-balance, hoping to give the assassin another opportunity to strike. Basil rolled on the stone floor, wrenching his arm from André's grip, and sprung back to his feet. Even in torchlight, André could see his brother's blood staining the cold stones.

The assassin and Basil crouched, assessing each other. When the man thrust the knife, Basil swept his uninjured arm upward, knocking it from the man's hand, and sending it sliding across the floor to slam against the wall. Weaponless, the assassin ran. Basil started after him, but limped so badly he gave up the chase.

When André saw his brother coming towards him, he started singing drunkenly, waving his arms in the air. A door opened cautiously and a head poked out.

"Go back to sleep," his brother said to the man. "It's all over."

Basil grabbed one arm and dragged André to his bedchamber door.

"Let me go, you swine."

Basil pounded loudly until the manservant answered the door.

"Put your drunken master to bed."

As Basil turned away, André glanced up from his place on the floor. The assassin botched the killing of his brother, putting himself and Courbet at grave risk.

He cursed long and loudly.

Basil limped to his chamber and roused his manservant. He accepted aid removing his sliced clothing and leaned wearily over the table. In the light of multi-branched candelabra, the manservant cleansed the wounds.

The slice across his back was superficial so the servant wrapped the wound with cloth strips, securing moldy bread and herbal salve over the injury.

The wound on his arm was deeper. Basil had stemmed the blood flow with pressure so now it barely oozed. The servant washed it with linen cloth dipped in water warmed by the fireplace. Basil drank eagerly from a flagon of wine as the servant prepared catgut and needle to sew the ragged edges together.

"My half-brother got drunk and caused a disturbance in the Hall," he told the servant.

"Again?"

"Drunk, loud and obnoxious. I got him out of there before he did too much damage."

"Did he do this to you?"

"No. Before I could get my brother to his chamber tonight, I was attacked."

"By his friends?" the manservant asked.

"No. A felon wanting revenge. He accused me of false imprisonment."

Basil bit down on wood and pounded the table to keep from crying out while his servant sewed the eight stitches to close the wound. Sweat stood out on his forehead and his heart pounded in his ears until the wound was finally bound.

Gratefully, he finished off the wine and allowed the servant to dress him for bed.

"Two against one," the servant said. "No wonder they got the better of you."

"My brother had already fallen down. Drunk," Basil said as he stretched out on the bed. "Unfortunately, we'd fought earlier and André kicked my knee. I couldn't react fast enough."

"I'll wrap your knee in vinegar compresses. It'll take the swelling down."

"The felon left his knife behind. Maybe I can use it to trace him."

"God's mercy you're safe."

I can't breathe.

A large, rough, smelly hand clamped securely over Lynnet's mouth and nose as she was awakened from a deep sleep. Other hands kept her arms and legs from flailing, defeating any thought of struggle against the force holding her down onto her bed.

"Knock her out," a gruff voice whispered. "If she screams and wakes up that other one, there'll be hell to pay."

The pain of the blow shocked her. Sparks flew around inside her head. When they settled down, darkness was everywhere.

Chapter Sixteen

Rowing. Out of a jumble of disorganized thought, Lynnet gleaned the awareness of a rocking motion. She was wrapped tightly, her arms down at her sides, the rough cloth pushing against her mouth, making it difficult to breathe.

I'm in a small boat. I'm wrapped in a rug again.

Her head hurt abominably. She felt nauseous and prayed she would not vomit. There was no place for the vomit to go. She would choke on it.

Fear rose. Trapped and helpless, her heart beat erratically. Its wild panic echoed in reverberations in her pounding head. Despair overwhelmed her as she sank gratefully back into unconsciousness.

Basil awoke grudgingly to the pounding on his door. His body ached like he was a loser in a jousting match.

"What now? Can't I be left alone?"

The fire had burned down to embers. It was even too early for his manservant to build a new one.

"It's the crack of dawn."

He threw back the bedding and checked his knee. The swelling had gone down. He could bend it.

Basil hung his legs over the side of the bed and waited. He

wanted to be certain there was no dizziness left from last night's loss of blood.

Forgetting about the injured arm, he briskly drew back the heavy velvet bed drape. Pain shot into his shoulder and down through his fingers when the wounded site struck the bedpost.

The pounding on the door continued.

"Hold your horses. I'm coming."

He swept a hand under the bed, searching for his boots. His manservant had strict orders to stow them there, in readiness for urgent situations.

Basil drew the boots on, threw a heavy cloak around his shoulders to ward off the chilled air and made his way unsteadily across the room.

"What is it?" he grumbled.

Only when the door was half open did he remember he'd left his weapons on the table.

Isolda stood in the shadowed doorway, her plump face distorted by anxiety.

"My lady is gone. She disappeared during the night."

Basil froze. His stomach clenched.

I thought they would come after me, not her.

"When?"

"We don't know. She was missing when I came to stoke the fire."

"Come in. Tell me what you know while I get dressed."

She stepped inside and closed the door as Basil grabbed his pants and tunic from the chest. He sat on the bed and removed his boots to pull on his pants. He flung off the cloak to slip on his linen tunic, then replaced the heavy wool cloak and boots. He hung his Seal of Office around his neck.

Isolda was wringing her hands.

"I should've slept in the chamber until Evelyn was well."

And I should have posted a guard at her door the whole night.

"There's no sign the door was forced."

"Could she have sleepwalked?"

The servant slumped onto a chair without asking permission.

"Her parents say no. No one in their family sleepwalks."

"What about her companion?"

"Evelyn's unharmed. She'd taken a sleeping potion. She didn't hear a thing."

Basil walked to the table where his belt and weapons were laid out. He lifted the cloak high enough to clamp the belt around his waist and methodically attach weapons to thongs and sheaths.

He headed for the door.

"Come on. Let's get over there."

The Tower was barely stirring. A feeble red streak at the horizon was all to be seen of dawn. A few retainers passed. Intent on their own duties, they paid scant attention to the sheriff and Isolda as they dashed towards Lady Lynnet's bedchamber.

A rooster crowed. Others joined him.

Don't greet this cursed dawn with cheer.

Loss defined in sharp detail Lynnet's value. Vigorous, proudly Norman, he had fallen in love with a Saxon, a woman the world saw as flawed and weak. He knew her strength, the calm serenity of her soul.

She deserves better than me, but I love her beyond understanding.

The circuitous path leading him from suspicion of Saxons to desiring a Saxon woman as the core of his life could not be traced by logic. Somehow, in the past weeks, his eyes opened. Truths he held dear since childhood crumbled. Black-and-white justifications acquired nuances. Beliefs had shifted.

Because of the altercation with his brother, he ended up weakened and lax in duty. Her disappearance was his fault. If he had been uninjured, he would have remembered to station a guard all night for Lynnet.

His heart felt gouged out.

When Basil and Isolda arrived at Lynnet's bedchamber, the door was standing open.

"Our daughter is kidnapped. Again," her father said as he paced the floor in agitation still wearing his bed clothes.

Isolda and he entered and Basil secured the door behind himself. He didn't want anyone walking the corridor to overhear.

"They took her in her night clothes," Evelyn said, looking distraught.

"What are you going to do about it?" Her mother's lace nightcap sat askew on disheveled hair.

Basil concentrated all his willpower so as not to throw furnishings against the wall in frustration. He wanted to tear something or somebody apart with his bare hands, but patience and methodical thought were needed now.

He looked around the room. The door showed no sign of force. Bedding was neatly folded back as if Lynnet had merely gotten up and walked off. There was no sign of disturbance. He turned to Isolda.

"You said you were the first to see she was missing?"

"I was."

"Is this bedding as you found it?"

"Yes.

"And the drapery was tied back out of the way?"

"She always slept with that side open," Evelyn said from where she lay on the trundle bed. "If she needed to get up during the night, she didn't want to get entangled in the draperies."

"There's no sign of a struggle," her father said.

"Nothing was stolen either," Isolda said. "Evelyn and I looked."

"Could she have needed something in the night and gone out to get it? Gotten lost?"

"Unlikely," Evelyn said. "She wakes me if she needs anything."

"And you heard nothing?"

"Nothing. I'd taken a sleeping potion."

Basil's irritation increased. He wanted to race through the castle shouting for Lynnet, but asking tame questions was the best way to find her.

"What about the bar? Don't you bar the door at night?"

"No. The door was locked with a key," Evelyn said.

"At home we don't need to lock our doors," her father reminded him.

"The key was out of the lock and hung by the door as you see it," Evelyn said, "so Isolda could get in with her own key in the morning."

The kidnappers had a key from their first attempt. I should have insisted the door be barred instead of assuming it!

His stupidity flooded acid into his stomach until he winced.

"Why are you wasting time?" her mother said testily. "Why don't you go out and start looking?"

Basil's temper snapped. He strode over to Lady Durwyn, dwarfing her by his size.

"Sit down and stay out of my way! No one will look harder for your daughter than I will!"

"You dare speak to me like that?" her mother sputtered.

Nonetheless, she sat herself rigidly in a straight chair by the fire, looking incensed. Her unobtrusive husband took a stool nearby.

Candle in hand, Basil searched the chamber, head bowed down to look for anything dropped or footprints.

Not even one muddy footprint.

Her abductors must have come from inside the Tower because outside the ground was still slush. Either that or they wore cloth sacks over their shoes.

Cloth would've cut down on noise too.

He'd send guards to interrogate those staying along the corridor in the hope someone had heard or seen something.

Basil searched the bedding. The abductors left nothing behind.

"It's made to look like she sleepwalked or decided to go someplace on her own."

"She never would," Evelyn said.

"I believe you."

"If only I had woken up," she wailed.

"They would have abducted you as well."

"At least my lady would not be alone."

The despair in her voice plunged Basil's spirit down.

Someone clever planned this abduction. Count Maximilian was devious, but he was in Wessex. André seemed unlikely, being heavy-handed by nature and falling-down drunk last night. It was probably the third conspirator.

Basil slammed the candle holder on the table with a crash and strode towards the door. He'd confront his brother.

"I'll alert the Captain of the Guards," he said over his shoulder as he flung open the door, "and arrange for search parties."

My brother will give me that third name or else.

Lynnet woke up with a sputter. Water was pouring into her nose and mouth. She broke the surface and gulped in large breaths of air before being dragged under again.

A strong current moved her along.

I've been thrown into the Thames.

Cold was eating into her. If she didn't act quickly, she'd soon add to the river's foul smell.

At least, on the boat I was wrapped in a warm rug.

Panicking, she paddled arms and legs furiously to push up and out of the water. Debris struck her from all sides. Breaking the surface, she gulped in air, feeling rivulets stream down her chilled face.

They want me dead.

"Help! Help!"

Chapter Seventeen

Basil pounded on André's chamber door. A sleepy manservant answered. The sheriff pushed past him towards the bed where his half-brother was just waking up. He grabbed André by his nightshirt and dragged him upright. The pulse behind Basil's temples pounded erratically. Fury rose from his gut, forming a heated knot behind his Adam's apple.

"Where is she? What have you done with her?"

"Unhand me."

"Lady Lynnet has disappeared. I know you and your vicious friends are behind it."

His brother threw a punch, which landed on Basil's chin, snapping his head back, and loosening his grip. Taking the advantage, André pushed him away and sprang out of bed.

Basil regained his balance, grabbed his half-brother and spun him around, demanding, "Who is working with you? Who took her?"

André twisted from his grasp.

"Let's settle this outside, like gentlemen, instead of brawling like those tavern louts where you grew up."

André started pulling on his trousers, his back brazenly to the sheriff.

Basil grabbed his half-brother around the throat, pulling

him against his body, his forearm wrapped tightly against André's windpipe.

"You'll tell me now where she is."

Defiant, a rasp in his voice and struggling for air, André said, "I don't know what you're talking about."

His fingers tore at Basil's forearm.

Soldiers stationed in the hallway rushed into the chamber and Basil pushed his half-brother towards them. The manservant cowered in a corner.

"A cell will loosen your tongue."

André snarled and cursed as the two burly men twisted his arms behind his back and force-marched him out the opened door.

"Son of a whore, you can't do this."

"I act under the authority of the king. Tell me the name of the third man and seek the king's mercy."

André spit at his brother.

"My father will kill you."

"If Lady Lynnet dies, I'll see you pay with your life, whether under the law or not."

Matilda was almost overpowered by the gloom emanating from Lynnet's chamber when Isolda opened the door. She and Geoff had come to invite her friend to break her fast with them.

"What's wrong?"

"Lady Lynnet is missing."

Matilda's throat constricted and pressure built behind her eyes. She hurriedly dragged Geoff inside the chamber and closed the door.

"When?"

"We don't know exactly," Evelyn said from a chair near the fireplace. Her face was ashen, her eyes drawn. "Sometime during the night. I had taken a sleeping draught. I didn't hear a thing."

"God's wounds."

Matilda sank onto a nearby stool. Geoff knelt, wrapping his arms around her.

"We notified the sheriff," Isolda said. "He's organizing search parties."

Matilda shuddered. Only months before, a search party was looking for her. Too injured to walk and deep in a forest, it was sheer luck that she'd been found.

Geoff got up.

"I'd better find Basil. He'll need all the help he can get."

Matilda saw her husband to the door. She kissed him on the lips.

"Bring her back safely."

After Geoff left, Matilda turned to the two women. She ran her fingers through the mass of curls on the top of her head.

"How could this have happened?"

"We don't know," Evelyn said, wringing her hands. "The door was locked last night."

"The sheriff checked. It wasn't forced," Isolda said. "If we didn't know better, it would look like she just got up and walked away."

"She'd never intentionally cause us worry," Evelyn said.

Matilda sat on the high-backed chair on the opposite side of the fireplace from Evelyn. Isolda stood near the bed, her hand grabbing tightly onto the bedpost.

"What about her parents?" Matilda asked.

"They went back to their chamber after the sheriff left," Evelyn said. "For once, they looked upset for their daughter."

"What can we do?" Isolda asked. "I'm going crazy with worry. I need something to do with my hands."

"For one thing, we can get water hot for a bath and warm some cider," Matilda said. "A couple months ago, I was lost in the woods. When found, what I wanted most, besides Geoff, was a warm blanket and hot food."

"That's right," Evelyn said. "We should prepare for Lynnet's return."

Isolda headed for the door.

"I'll go to the kitchen for food. I'll have a tub and water sent up."

Evelyn picked up the poker, turning over embers before adding firewood.

"I'll get this fire going better."

"And I'll choose clean clothes," Matilda said, "and bring more blankets."

Despite the cold eating into her body, Lynnet was thankful for her lighter-weight nightclothes and bare feet. If she'd been wearing multi-layers of clothing and her shoes, she'd be dragged to the bottom by now.

She paddled, sluggishly, managing to keep her head above water except for stray splashes churned up by the wind. Her father was to be thanked for lessons in swimming when, after losing her vision, he feared she would fall into the estate pond and drown.

"You can't get away with this," she muttered through chattering teeth towards the far off sounds of a rowboat. "Somehow I'll survive." She touched her crystal where it was caught in the folds of her bodice.

Her abductors hadn't bothered to bind her wrists.

They want this to look like an accident!

They hadn't stayed around to watch her die either.

They don't know I can swim.

Something slammed roughly into the crown of her head. Her face dipped briefly underwater. Sputtering, she felt around and grabbed a slimy, somewhat rotted surface. With her hands, she determined its size and shape.

"Blessed Providence. A timber beam."

Using the wood's buoyancy, she pulled her head and shoulders as high as possible out of the water, ignoring the biting morning air.

Night was quickly giving way to dawn as grayed shapes differentiated themselves along the shoreline. She must have been in that rowboat for a long time if a new day was already dawning. Her captors probably rowed her far enough from the Tower to make a nearby search useless.

"Surely, with morning light, someone will find me."

She prayed it would be Basil. The first voice she wanted to hear upon being dragged from these unholy waters was his. She clung to the memory of his kiss to ward off black despair.

If she survived, she'd declare her love.

Not if. When.

Chapter Eighteen

Basil hadn't decided yet if he'd done his half-brother a disservice. It was only now that, while he ran from the bedchamber to the Great Hall, his temper cooled and reason reasserted itself.

It was entirely possible André had nothing to do with Lynnet's disappearance. Still, his half-brother had something to do with the thefts and the plotting against Saxons. A day in a cell might soften him up. Problems with his father over this jailing couldn't be contemplated. Basil had no energy to spare.

"I'll worry about whether I was fair to André later. Now, I have to see how many men were rounded up for search parties."

Lord Wilfgive suffered the loss of one child to sickness. Now, his remaining child might be lost to him. His shoulders slumped. He sank back into a chair in his Tower chamber. The first rays of dawn were struggling through the unshuttered window.

"Tragedy forces one to differentiate between what is important and what is frivolous," he said to his wife, his heart heavy.

"Are you getting philosophical on me?"

"I should have been more attentive to Lynnet's needs. I

should've given more credence to her experiences in the cellar." A sadness for opportunities lost welled up, constricting his throat. "She's been showing a preference for this Norman sheriff. I should've given her my blessing."

"You can't be serious."

Lord Wilfgive leaned across the table and patted his wife's hand.

"We must think of Lynnet's happiness. She deserves better when she's returned to us."

"But he has no money."

"We do, my dear."

"But he's Norman."

"So is the king. And Basil is the acknowledged son of the Earl of Chester. The earl will certainly give him an adequate living if he marries well."

His tone was deliberately conciliatory. Over the years, he'd learned this was the best way to handle his volatile wife.

"I've come to believe our daughter really did overhear a conspiracy and that's why she was kidnapped again."

His wife shrugged her shoulders. "I was sure she was having one of her hallucinations."

"A reasonable assumption."

"When upset, she's prone to seeing things."

He smiled as memories of his mother came to mind.

"Imagining her dear grandmother must bring her comfort."

"She probably chose your mother deliberately to irk me. The two of us never got along."

"I'm afraid our daughter is in terrible trouble."

Lady Durwyn sprang from her chair, knocking it backwards to crash on the floor.

"You have to do something. She's my only hope for grandchildren."

He rose and put his arms around his beloved wife, pressing her head against his shoulder.

"There, there. It'll all turn out right. I'll see to it."

"How?"

"I'll go to the king. He'll look for our daughter. He'll rouse all of London if need be."

Basil nodded approval upon seeing the number of men milling about in the Great Hall. The din of raised voices reverberated off stone walls. Curious children were gathered up and ordered to play in a corner, out of the men's way. Dogs ran underfoot. Soldiers shouted orders, directing men into groups. Basil hailed the Captain of the Guard and strode over to him.

"How goes it?"

"I've chosen three sergeants to lead the searches. All our hunt dogs have been rounded up."

Basil glanced towards the men shouting orders. They appeared to know their jobs.

"So I see."

"One is in charge of the grounds, another the castle and the last will organize a search of the river banks."

Basil's stomach lurched. There was always thc chance Lynnet would never be found. And another that she would be found dead.

He shook himself and focused on the search preparations.

Such thoughts do me no good.

Unconsciously, he checked that his short sword was in place at his side.

"I can't be everywhere. How will I get word when she's found?"

"I'm staying in the Hall," the Captain said. "All news will be relayed to me. Let me know where you'll be and I'll get word to you."

Satisfied that the search preparations were in good hands, Basil left the Hall after telling the Captain that he could be found in the Treasury. Earlier, he'd sent a messenger to summon Nicolas to the Tower. Basil needed to find out what the spies had learned about his brother's recent activity. He desperately wanted to learn the identity of the third man.

"Sir André's been thrown in jail," Count Courbet's man hissed at him as he opened his chamber door.

"Get in here."

The count dragged the man roughly by the arm into the chamber and firmly shut the door. He spun him around to face him.

"What's this?"

"Instead of killing his brother, Sir André is in a cell. The sheriff struck first."

Courbet's chest constricted. He found it hard to breathe. His heartbeat rose alarmingly.

"That bastard son of a whore. I never thought he'd have the guts to touch us." He cursed. "André assured me he wouldn't act against Norman lords, especially not against his father's son."

"What will you do?"

Courbet's mind whirled with conflicting courses of action. He ran his fingers through his thick hair.

"I'll go to France."

"France?"

His manservant's face looked stricken, probably because he'd be leaving his family behind.

"I can't trust André to curb his tongue. When you order our horses saddled, say I'm visiting a relative for a few days. It's important no one realizes we aren't coming back."

"Yes, my lord."

Courbet rushed towards the door.

"I need to get my valuables and papers from the Treasury."

"Shall I start packing?"

He halted and glared at his servant.

"No. No baggage. Only food and water and a change of clothes in the saddle bags. We can buy what we need before we get on a boat."

"Yes, my lord."

"Meet me at the stables within the half hour."

Evelyn, Matilda and Isolda were at loose ends. Water and cider were heating, clean clothes and blankets at ready and slices of cheese with hunks of fresh bread were crowded onto a metal platter. The bathing tub was tucked in a corner behind an ornate screen. The several buckets of water in it were coming to room temperature as the women waited for news.

Matilda and Evelyn sat on chairs at the table and Isolda on a wooden stool by the fireplace. Each had a steaming mug of ale.

"I've been her teacher and companion since she was eight years old," Evelyn said, trying to break the silence that descended once chores were done. "She's very intelligent."

"A sensible head on her shoulders," Isolda agreed.

"But with a tendency to take too many chances," Matilda added.

The other women nodded their heads.

Matilda reached for a piece of cheese. "I've known Lynnet only a couple of weeks. Does she panic in emergencies?"

"Just the opposite," Evelyn said, after swallowing a bite of bread. "Considering her lack of sight, she has a very cool head."

"I thought she was developing an affection for the sheriff," Matilda said.

"I wondered about that myself," Evelyn said. "She was paying more attention to her clothes and jewelry."

"I wish she had warm clothes on now," Isolda said.

Evelyn caught her breath.

"I can't tell you how terrible I feel that my sleeping potion allowed her abduction to take place."

Tears welled up behind her eyes and threatened to spill out.

"Don't blame yourself," Matilda said. "They'd have found some way to get at her."

"If they took her out of the Tower," Isolda said, "we may never find her."

The women were quiet for a long time after that. The only sounds were those of eating. Each had to find her own reason to try to find hope.

Chapter Nineteen

The strain of Lynnet's disappearance was starting to tell. Basil wanted to be with the men looking for her, but duty lay with the king. Solving one problem might solve the other.

Although the sun was barely risen, the informant was wide awake and already seated in the anteroom of the Treasury when Basil arrived. He closed the door to keep their conversation from the ears of the guards and dropped down onto a chair, weary.

"What do you have for me, Nicolas?"

"I saw the one I believe to be the third man, but he was in shadows when talking with your brother at midday meal yesterday. I couldn't identify him."

Basil's shoulders drooped from disappointment. He rubbed his forehead.

"I was in the Great Hall then. I missed them."

Nicolas grunted. "I'm used to sneaking around. If they'd seen someone your size coming, they'd have split up before anything could be heard. Your kind is needed when the fighting begins."

The sheriff laughed in spite of himself.

"It's a good thing you're in your job and I'm in mine."

"They seemed to be arguing. I was prevented from following

the man because I was assigned to your half-brother."

"A description?"

Nicolas scratched his head.

"As tall as you, but not as broad. Definitely Norman and wearing jeweled rings. He carried himself well."

"That describes any number of the king's guests."

Basil shifted his weight. He had hoped for something better. His disappointment weighed heavy on his heart.

"It's important to know who he is. Lady Lynnet's been abducted. He may have arranged it."

The informant looked alarmed.

"I have to believe she's still alive," Basil said. "It's my fault. I was fighting with my brother when I should've been protecting her."

Nicolas grinned. "I hear he's in a cell. I'm sorry to say this because he's your family, but that's where he belongs."

Basil smiled grimly.

"I've thought that myself many times."

"I understand the chamberlain has been doing favors for him at great benefit to his pocketbook."

"I wonder if he's the one who gave the key to the abductors? There was no forced entry."

"I can find out for you."

"Do that."

"If I see that third man again, I'll know him by his manner. I'll follow him for you."

"Fine. And send word to me right away. I'll want to question him."

Basil rose to indicate the meeting was over. Since he was closest to the door, he reached out and opened it. Nicolas grabbed his arm, stopping him before it was fully open. The informant had a finger to his lips and motioned to re-shut the door.

"That's the man," Nicolas whispered. "That's the one who met with your brother."

Basil took a quick look before quietly closing the door.

"Count Courbet de Shereborne."

"Should we confront him?"

"He's from a powerful family, but I don't see where I have any choice."

Basil opened the door and discovered Courbet was gone. He went over to the guards.

"What did the count want?"

The guard saluted, then answered, "He had a box stored here. He's visiting relatives for a couple of days and needed it with him."

"Like hell he's visiting relatives. He's about to flee."

Basil turned and sprinted to the corridor. He cleared the door and looked both ways. No one was in sight. Once again he was too slow.

"Hell's bells."

Nicolas turned to the guard. "Did he name his chamber when he left the box?"

"He's staying in the Laurel Room."

"Come on," Basil yelled as he raced down the hallway.

Lynnet was becoming sleepy as she was rocked up and down on the wooden beam. The cold numbed her whole body. Her breathing seemed to be slowing down. Afraid she might fall asleep and slip off, she hiked her nightgown up near her hips and knotted both ends underneath to tie herself to the beam.

The skin on her head stretched tight as the goose egg caused from being knocked out pushed relentlessly against the hair, pounding and aching. She closed her eyelids to concentrate the pain away. With the dawn, boats of trade came onto the river.

"Surely someone will find me then."

She wanted Basil's arms to lift her from these waters before they became her tomb.

"Foolish. How will he know where I am?"

No one may even know she was missing. It seemed like hours since she awoke with the shock of cold water, but, probably, it was mere minutes. The sun was not fully risen.

Taking a risk, she released one hand from the beam. She felt along the silver chain at her neckline to touch her crystal pendant.

Lord Wilfgive's mare galloped around a bend in the road. He was relieved when Westminster Palace came into sight. Long trips by horse were hard on him now he was older.

He had to admit that the king's new residence was magnificent bathed in the red tones of sunrise. His scholarly indulgences gave him an appreciative eye. Each time he saw it, he was overwhelmed by its architectural beauty.

He slowed his horse. As it trotted towards the front entrance, he instructed the two guards riding with him to take their horses to the stables to feed, water and rub them down for the return journey.

After the guards left, he rode the short distance to where a young lad, dressed in the king's colors, stood. The stable boy assisted Lord Wilfgive to dismount, then walked the horse towards the stables.

Thankful to be on solid ground, he strode on unsteady legs up the stairs to the entrance. He spoke to the guard on duty.

"Lord Wilfgive of Osfrith requests an audience with the king."

The guard bowed, acknowledging the nobleman's rank.

"The king is breaking his fast. I'll send a page to learn when he can see you."

"It is an urgent matter."

The guard summoned a page and instructed the youth to carry the message. He turned back to Lynnet's father.

"My lord, may I escort you to a chamber to await the king."

Lord Wilfgive tottered wearily after the guard who led the way to a chamber near the Great Hall.

As he entered the small room, he nodded approval at a chair whose curved arms ended in cat paws. In his own home, he had furniture of this quality.

Settling gratefully into a cushioned chair, he glanced out the arched windows at the November day. The recent snowy days aggravated his arthritis. He was grateful for the fire burning hotly in the fireplace.

Only my dear wife could get me out on a day like this.

Not having removed his outer garments, Lord Wilfgive became overheated. He was almost asleep, his head drooping towards his chest, by the time the king and his deputy arrived.

"Greetings, Wilfgive," King Henry said upon entering. "You remember my deputy, Baron Otheur?"

"I do."

Her father rose to greet the king and his deputy.

"Take your ease," the king said, motioning him back into

the chair.

Wilfgive gratefully sank back down onto the cushioned seat.

"What brings you to Westminster so unexpectedly?" the deputy asked in his direct manner.

"My daughter is missing."

"Lynnet?" the king exclaimed as he took his seat behind the table. "When?"

"Sometime last night. The maidservant discovered her missing when she came at dawn to stoke the fire."

The deputy turned to King Henry.

"You warned Sheriff Basil something like this might happen."

The king pressed the heel of his hand to his forehead as if an ache were developing behind it.

"Has the sheriff formed a search party?"

Lynnet's father nodded his head.

"But Lady Durwyn doesn't believe he has the resources to find her. She wants the army called out."

The expression first appearing on the king's face was one of incredulousness. It was quickly replaced by a controlled, bland look. He turned to his deputy.

"Ride to the Tower at once. Place the full power of my authority behind this search."

"Right away, Your Majesty."

The deputy bowed then left the chamber.

Relief flooded through Lord Wilfgive. His wife would get what she wanted. All of London would be looking for their daughter.

King Henry returned his attention to him.

“What would you say to hot, mulled wine before your return journey?”

Count Courbet rushed about his chamber grabbing small things he didn’t want to leave behind. The valuables and papers went into a soft, leather pouch to keep them from prying eyes.

He glanced hurriedly around the room.

“What a shame to leave my best clothes.”

Shrugging his shoulders, he forced himself to come to grips with an uncertain future.

“It was the game we played. We lost.”

He strode quickly across the chamber floor. As he flung open the heavy door, the blood in his veins chilled at hearing the sheriff’s voice.

“Where do you think you’re going?”

Chapter Twenty

When the door opened unexpectedly, Basil's short sword was angled towards Count Courbet's throat. The sheriff got out one challenge before the conspirator threw the leather pouch he was carrying at him and rammed his head into Basil's chest. Only the sheriff's bulk and a wide stance kept him from tumbling backwards. Even so, the short sword clattered to the floor.

Courbet's muscular arms grabbed him in a bear hug, thrusting him outward into the corridor. Pushed off balance, Basil took three steps backwards before wrapping his own brawny arms around Courbet, taking them both to the stone floor.

Each man struggled for dominance. Muscle strained against muscle as they rolled back and forth. Legs lashing out, hands gripping tightly to Courbet's tunic, Basil fought to restrain this man responsible for Lynnet's disappearance. He could not let him get away again.

The man's hot, sour breath poured over him and as the conspirator pushed closer as if to bite off an ear, Basil twisted his head away.

Suddenly, Courbet's snarling face collapsed and his body sprawled across Basil like a dead man. The sheriff looked up. Standing above them was Nicolas, the heavy, wooden stick he wore tied to his belt raised in his hands, a big grin on his face.

"Sometimes even a big warrior like you can use a little help from a skinny guy like me."

Basil grinned in spite of himself.

"Let's get this piece of garbage to a cell."

Lynnet knew she was drifting in and out of grogginess. Sometimes she had a hard time remembering where she was. Only the draining cold reminded her.

As she clung to the beam, she became aware of her grandmother's presence floating above the water. A sense of well-being came over her. She was not alone.

"Do you know what I regret, Grandmamma? I regret that I never married. I regret not knowing a man's love."

As if her grandmother spoke, Lynnet absorbed the thought, *"You have a man you love."*

Lynnet smiled.

"You're right. I have a man I love."

She drifted, peacefully, for a few moments.

"Do you know what, Grandmamma? I don't care what my parents say. I don't care if I must sell all my jewels and live in rags. I'll find some way to convince Basil to marry me."

As Lynnet again slowly lost consciousness, she dreamed of making love to Basil.

Chapter Twenty-One

When Basil and Nicolas dragged the unconscious count to a cell, the sheriff was astounded to find the king's deputy in the Tower cellars.

"Don't look so surprised," Baron Otheur said. "Lord Wilfgive convinced the king to become involved."

"You know Lady Lynnet is missing?"

The baron nodded.

"I stopped at the Hall on my way down here and got a full report. The captain seems to be handling matters."

Basil released his grip, letting Courbet drop, still unconscious, onto the stone floor. Nicolas stood guard over him with his wooden stick.

"Here's your third conspirator."

The Baron's eyes widened.

"Count Courbet de Shereborne?"

"I was just about to interrogate him."

The baron summoned soldiers. They picked up the unconscious count under both arms.

"Put him in a cell."

As the soldiers dragged Courbet away, the deputy said, "Leave that one to me. And your brother too."

"Our father doesn't know of his treachery."

"Don't say a word. Wait until I get answers."

Basil's spirit lifted. Heavy burdens were rolling off his shoulders. The deputy's next words made his heart sing.

"Join the search. I'll take over from here on out. When I get your brother and that one to talk," the king's deputy said, "you'll have a better chance of finding her."

All he'd wanted to do since dawn was search for Lynnet. Duty to the king interfered. Now, the baron assumed that duty, releasing Basil's pent-up frustrations.

As he turned towards the Hall, his informant caught his arm. "I'll take a soldier to arrest the chamberlain."

Basil nodded.

"You're a good man, Nicolas."

"We don't want any of them to get away."

"You may have saved my life today. At the least, you saved me from embarrassment."

"You owe me."

Basil was almost to the end of the corridor when he heard Baron Otheur call out, "By the by, we got word that Count Maximilian is dead."

"By my man's hand?"

"No. Thieves. Ironic, isn't it?"

Basil's thoughts dwelt on Lynnet as he jogged towards the Hall. He hoped fate would not be cruel and reveal love only to snatch it away forever.

Paradoxically, his drunken brother was the catalyst. While their fight resulted in the physical loss of his love because he hadn't posted a guard, it also created the circumstances for the astounding recognition of that love.

He would ask Lynnet to marry him. He didn't have wealth, but no man would try harder to make her happy.

"I have to find her."

Chapter Twenty-Two

Lynnet awoke to shouting. Through the grogginess, she distinguished human voices and the lapping sounds of water against the wooden sides of a boat. Hope surged.

She twisted her head towards the sounds. Among the shadows, she picked out a dark shape bearing down on her. She smelled the pungent odor of dung.

It must be one of those barges moving human waste downriver to farmlands.

She barely made out the shapes of two boatmen gesturing for her to get out of the way.

"Help. Help. I'm blind."

The barge would run her down and she would drown if she chose the wrong direction. She quickly unknotted her nightgown from the beam and turned her head from side to side, trying to decide. Her heart beat erratically, seeming to want to break through her chest wall. Then it took a leap of joy. Her grandmother's apparition appeared to her right.

"Grandmamma."

Lynnet let go of the beam pulling her into the path of the barge and paddled towards the vision of her grandmother. Her arms and legs felt lethargic from the cold. The water's drag as the barge slowly slid past stretched her clothing and hair out upon the water behind her. She redoubled her efforts. *I can't get dragged under.*

A metal hook entangled with her clothing. Lynnet screamed.

"Lord have mercy."

She was being lifted out of the water and swung through the air. She hit the side of the barge with a clunk.

"Hang on," a male voice shouted.

Breathless and shivering, Lynnet grasped the wooden railing as best she could. The movement of the barge dragged her legs underneath it, threatening to pull her away. She dug her fingernails into the rough wood and prayed.

"Hang on. I'm putting the boat hook down."

Lynnet felt the long pole being set against the barge, its metal hook still entangled in her clothing.

"I'm coming to get you."

Strong hands clasped her underarms, jerking her totally out of the frigid water, and dropping her onto the rough planking of the barge. The boat hook ripped from her clothing and fell to the floor with a clang.

"Stay there. I have to get back to the tiller."

"I'll stay."

Lynnet shivered in the cold morning air, thankful to be alive. She lay, trying to catch her breath. The stench of drying cattle and human dung assailed her nostrils.

"What were you doing in the river?"

This voice was different. This was not the man who pulled her from the waters. She turned her head and vaguely made out against the morning sky a man working a long pole. Lynnet felt the barge change direction slightly.

"Someone tried to kill me. I was grabbed from my bed and tossed into the Thames."

"You're lucky you're not dead."

"I know."

"We have no blankets. In a quarter hour's time, we will arrive at where we live. We'll give you dry clothing then."

"She can have my cloak," the man at the tiller said as he came towards her.

A smelly, rough, wool cloak enveloped her. She wrapped it tightly around and believed she had never felt anything as comforting in her life.

"I am Lady Lynnet of Osfrith," she said, her teeth chattering. "Second cousin to the late queen. Return me to my family at the Tower and you'll be rewarded for your kindness."

Basil was next to the Captain of the Guard when the deputy's courier arrived with the news that Courbet confessed that Lady Lynnet was dead and thrown into the Thames.

Black rage enveloped Basil. His heart squeezed to near bursting. His gut wrenched with anguished grief. He'd lost the promise of love before he had a chance to experience it.

"They'll pay for this," Basil said through gritted teeth. "I'll see they pay."

The evidence he'd gather would allow them no opportunity to use influence or money to escape justice. He'd make sure the king separated their heads from their shoulders.

"Call the soldiers back from the Tower and the woods," the captain was shouting to his sergeants. "Have them drag the river for the body."

Basil confronted the captain.

"I'll join the dragging of the river. I want to be there when she's found."

Geoff's voice as he called out while pounding on Lynnet's chamber door alerted Matilda that his news was bad. She cringed, blood pounding in her ears. She raced to the door and swung it open.

"They found her?"

Geoff shook his head.

"No, but Count Courbet confessed to having her murdered and thrown in the Thames."

"Nooooo," her mother shrieked as she jumped out of her chair and tore at her hair. She had arrived moments before to wait with those who loved Lynnet while her husband was gone to the king.

Isolda made the sign of the cross. Evelyn broke into racking sobs. Matilda flung herself into Geoff's arms.

"Oh, no. That can't be true. They can't have done such a despicable thing."

"Desperate men protect their own well-being," Geoff said, pressing her head against his shoulder. "She was a witness against them."

"That beautiful creature destroyed," Evelyn murmured, misery making her voice quiver.

"I'll go to the chapel to pray for her soul," Isolda said. She walked past the still-opened door, slowly, as if one of the walking dead.

"We'll leave this benighted abode," Lady Durwyn said, "as soon as our daughter's remains are recovered."

Geoff unclasped Matilda's hold arms from around his neck and gently set her away from him. He kissed her tenderly on the forehead.

"I'd better get back to the Hall," he said. "Basil is like a raging beast."

The sheriff bent his back into the task. He was knee-deep in cold, murky water near the Water Gate. Bottom silt, stirred up by the searcher's feet, made it impossible to see even an inch under the surface. But his task required precision, not sight. He needed to probe the river's depth inch by inch.

He chose this slice of riverbank near the Gate, believing that a hired hand would take the easy way out. He assumed Lynnet's assailant had sneaked past the guard and slipped his burden into the water as quickly as possible.

A multitude of footprints on the riverbank made it impossible to agree on where she had been discarded into the murky water. Instead, Basil had to work his way cautiously downstream, hoping that her body hadn't been dragged out into the current and swept away.

Muscles rippled across his back. The constant motion of flinging the heavy iron grappling hook out into the river, then pulling it back along the river bottom to the bank, tested his reserves of strength. Animal carcasses, broken furniture and pieces of wrecked boats were his only salvage so far. With each toss, he both feared and hoped he'd recover Lynnet. He worked with a fierce passion. At day's end, he wanted his body so exhausted, his mind so tired, he wouldn't remember.

"Basil. You'll kill yourself at this pace."

The sheriff looked up to see Lord Geoff coming towards him.

"You stink to high heaven." Geoff waved his hand in front of his nose. "Let the hired men do this gruesome task. Come away with me. Lord Otheur sent word for you to join him in interrogating your brother and Courbet."

Basil adamantly shook his head.

"Send my regrets."

"You'll jeopardize your position."

"None of that matters anymore."

Geoff turned and started back towards the castle.

"I'll word your regrets in such way that you can change your mind."

"I won't. I failed to protect her. I'll not fail her now. I'll find her, even if I have to live on this riverbank and search for the rest of my days."

Chapter Twenty-Three

Shivering despite the overly large, thick-wool, male clothing she was wearing, Lynnet sat huddled in the back of the lurching cart. She was excited to be traveling back to the Tower, drawing ever closer to Basil.

When the men had gotten the barge of dung to the farming community on the outskirts of London, they had taken her to their houseboat. There, they gave her dry clothing, fed her and were now acting as her bodyguards en route to the king's castle.

The rickety cart, drawn by a slow-moving horse, made its bumpy way over ruts caused by ice and thaw. The driver and the horse were familiar with this route from carrying freshly slaughtered meat along this road to the Tower three times a week.

It was good fortune indeed that the driver was a friend of the boatmen. Because of this, he was willing to wait for compensation until arrival at the Tower. Slow as the cart may be, it was still faster than rowing upstream. Besides, she quaked at the thought of any more water beneath her.

Since his friend refused to go to the Hall to eat, Lord Geoff lugged the basket of food and drink to him. Geoff also carried old clothing and boots. He hoped to convince Basil to leave the waters of the Thames long enough to warm himself at a courtyard fire.

"My impossible friend," Geoff yelled out as he got closer to the riverbank, "since you won't go to the food, I've brought the food to you."

"I'm not hungry."

"You can't help Lynnet if you're too tired to think straight. You might overlook something vital."

Geoff waited for the logic of the argument to sink in. He feared he'd lost when Basil didn't budge.

"Stop being stubborn. Come to the courtyard. There's a big bonfire going."

Basil just stood in the water looking lost.

"I've brought dry clothes and warm food. If you rest awhile, you'll be the better for it."

For a few moments, Geoff considered turning away in defeat. Eventually, Basil tossed the iron grappling hook onto the embankment at the place where he had finished searching and dragged himself up out of the water, exhaustion evident in his slow movements.

"You stink, my friend. I'll draw some water from the well so you can wash before changing clothes."

Dripping mucky sludge, Basil followed him with slow steps.

"You're a good friend," the sheriff said quietly. "I feel like I'm losing my mind."

"To help Lynnet, you must preserve your strength."

"You're right. Let's sit and eat."

The journey back to the Tower allowed Lynnet too much time to ponder. The more she thought, the less she could see why a vigorous man like Basil would tie himself to a wife with limited sight. Bad enough that she'd need help to run his household and prepare his food. Worse yet, she'd need help just to keep their children safe.

What does he get out of such a marriage?

It wasn't like her angry parents would help them financially.

She pressed her hands against the side of her temples, her elbows on her knees. Jumbled thoughts created pressure, starting her head to ache. She massaged her temples, closing her eyelids as if a sighted person needing to block the light.

When in the water and fearing death, she believed marrying Basil was her only reason to survive. On dry land, second thoughts reigned—she'd be a burden. Perhaps the greater love was to let him go.

A great depression of spirit fell over her.

"I would have married her," Basil said, his heart black with grief. "I'd made up my mind to ask her."

Now that he was warm and dry and replenishing his body with food, Basil felt the urge to explain about Lynnet. He and Geoff were sitting in the courtyard on the stone platform used to rest buckets of water drawn from the well. Geoff had laid a cloth between them with bread, cheese, meat and bladders of ale spread out on it.

"She would have married you," Geoff said, chewing on pork rind. "Despite her parents." He licked his fingers.

Basil reached for a hunk of cheese.

"I only realized I was in love when she went missing."

"That happened to me," Geoff said as he picked up a chicken leg. "I listed every logical reason not to marry Matilda, including my family's rejection of her. It was only when I thought I'd lost her that I realized the only important thing was our love."

Basil nodded his head in understanding. He, too, had done this. That was before he allowed his heart to take over.

"My quarters are small compared to what Lynnet is used to. It wouldn't have been easy for us."

"The way she brightened this past week when you came near, I don't think she'd have cared."

Basil bent over, elbows on knees, palms on his temples and his fingers entangled in his hair. Underneath a sick heart was intense rage. His half-brother was one of the men who destroyed his happiness.

"I would have done my best to see she was comfortable. Isolda would have helped run the household."

"And Evelyn would never have abandoned her," Geoff said. "That woman is like a mother to Lynnet."

When he heard footsteps, Basil looked up and saw a soldier coming towards them. The man stood at attention to report.

"Baron Otheur sends word," the soldier said solemnly. "The count confessed he had the lady rowed miles downstream. She was thrown overboard in the middle of the river so that she would not be found near the Tower by any search party."

Basil jumped up from the stone shelf, dragging the cloth and the food to the pavement with him. He threw back his head, fists aimed at the sky.

"I'll wring his worthless neck if the king does not cut it off first."

Chapter Twenty-Four

The cart had entered through one of the Tower gates from the road some minutes back, but the guard had directed them across the courtyard to the Water Gate where the search was centered. Lynnet heard the shouting as they rounded the base of the Tower.

"What's going on?"

"A bunch of armed men just came out of the Tower," the man at the reins said. "Another man is shaking his fists at the sky and shouting, but I can't hear what he's saying because of the noise."

"They must know you went into the river," a boatman said. "I see grappling hooks. They're trying to find your body."

Lynnet shivered as if someone were walking on her grave.

The cart jerked to a stop. She heard the two boatmen jump with a thump of boots onto the courtyard pavement. Lynnet stretched her arms and legs to relieve cramping. Surprisingly, after the cold, bumpy ride, her body parts still worked. Only her head and heart seemed malfunctioning. She hadn't resolved whether love meant clinging to Basil no matter what or letting him go for the greater good.

"My lady, if you'll wait here, we'll find someone to take you to your parents."

Butterflies flip-flopped in her stomach as the men walked away. All her back and forth thinking about Basil left her unsure. Her parents were adamant against him. Her heart wanted one thing, her head another.

And she was still not safe. Her enemies were staying at the Tower and could have seen her arrive. They might be looking at her right this minute. Lynnet turned her head slowly, concentrating, learning what she could from the bustling activity around her.

Her ear caught a sound and her heart leapt.

That voice is Basil's.

Her breath caught in her throat. Her heart beat erratically. An upwelling of happiness heated her whole body, creating a pleasurable prickling between her legs, pushing out any uncertainty.

Basil turned with annoyance as two dirty boatmen approached him and Lord Geoff.

"What do you want?"

He glanced briefly at the cart that had brought them into the courtyard to see if it carried anything dangerous. A boy sat with his back to Basil, but his posture was not threatening. The tired driver held the reins lightly. Basil recognized him as the butcher who brought meat to the castle. The horse was slumping as tiredly as its master.

When the boy turned his head, Lynnet's face peered out from underneath the hood of the heavy cloak. Wonder and joy enveloped him.

"Lynnet?"

Basil was already running as he heard the men explaining the circumstances to Geoff.

"We pulled a gentlewoman from the river. She's in danger and needs protection."

By the time Basil heard Geoff turn and run after him, he was already at the cart. He pulled Lynnet into his arms and kissed her frantically.

"I thought you were dead."

Raining desperate kisses over her chilled face and lips, he hugged her tightly to his chest so as never to lose her again. He exclaimed over and over, "I thought you were dead."

Lynnet's bosom crushed against a muscled chest. Her face lifted of its own accord to greet hot, breathy kisses showered over it by this demanding man. The dirt-matted beard and mustache tickled, bringing joyful awareness she was safely in the arms of her beloved. Reaching up, she ran probing fingertips across Basil's face, trying to convey the depth of her love. She stroked his beard and cheekbones before winding her arms possessively around his muscled neck.

"I love you." She whispered it into Basil's ear whenever an opportunity arrived.

Hugged so tightly, Lynnet found she had trouble breathing. It was as if Basil were proving to himself that she was flesh and blood and not an apparition like her grandmother.

He smelled ripe. As must she. The rank stench proved he'd been in the Thames searching for her.

When given a chance to breathe, she said, "Two boatmen saved my life."

"They will be rewarded."

"Have Evelyn bring a gold coin for each of them. And the driver needs to be paid."

"See to it," Lord Geoff said to the nearest soldier.

"We must let my parents know I'm alive."

"I'll see to it," Geoff said. She heard him walking away and giving instructions to several soldiers to inform the deputy, the Captain of the Guard, her parents and Matilda that she was safe.

"Marry me."

Lynnet's head held such a chaotic jumble of voices she couldn't believe she'd heard Basil's words.

"What?"

"I love you. Will you marry me?"

A smile spread, threatening to crack her chilled cheeks. She knew there must be others gathered near, listening, but she didn't care. This was not a moment for maidenly decorum.

"I love you more than life itself."

"Will you?"

"I will marry you and no other."

She felt herself gathered up and pressed against Basil's hard body as he strode towards the castle. His footsteps crunched on patches of icy snow.

"I'll inform your parents."

His heart pounded fiercely against her cheek through his heavy wool tunic. Physical evidence of his love pressed against her side as she bounced slightly with each step. Her body heated up. She cradled her head into his broad chest, feeling safe. Her fingers played with the fabric of his tunic.

"How did you stay alive?"

She heard the wonder in his voice.

"My abductors took me by boat, wrapped in a rug. It kept me warm."

Basil planted a quick kiss on her forehead.

"When I hit the cold water, I awoke from being knocked out."

"Bastards."

Lynnet shivered at the vehemence behind the word. She wouldn't want to be in the shoes of her abductors.

"A timber beam was nearby. I held on as it floated down river."

"A miracle."

"With the dawn, the bargemen saw me. They couldn't turn quickly and would have run me over had my grandmother not shown me the way to escape."

He didn't miss a step at the mention of her ghostly grandmamma.

"The men got me out of the water before I froze to death. They fed me on their houseboat and gave me dry clothing."

"I'll see they get some of the sheriff's business for their service to you."

Basil squeezed her tightly. "You're safe now. We've captured the conspirators. Two are in cells. One is dead. We're still looking for the hirelings who abducted you. They won't escape justice."

She reached up with one hand and stroked his cheekbone and beard.

"When in the water and thinking I might die, it was you I regretted losing most of all."

"I became a man possessed."

"I shouldn't allow you to saddle yourself to a woman lacking sight, but I intend to be utterly selfish."

"I have no right to ask you to sacrifice social standing by

marrying me." His voice sounded sad.

"Shhhh." She put her index finger against his lips. "It is but a little sacrifice."

"I'll make it my purpose to see you are happy every day of your life."

"No woman could ask for more."

Relief flooded through him as he carried Lynnet to her chamber. He hadn't realized he'd been holding his breath when waiting for her answer to his marriage proposal.

At first Basil thought Lynnet meant she loved him, but wouldn't marry him. It was only when he asked a second time that he knew she would become his wife.

Although he could have trained himself to accept whatever she offered, he desired the whole woman, not just words of love. He longed to start each day with Lynnet. He wanted the flesh and blood woman in his bed at night.

The door to Lynnet's bedchamber was open. A soldier was still delivering the message of her survival. When Basil made their presence known, her parents jumped up from where they'd been sitting at the table and rushed over. Her father, newly returned from the palace, kissed her cheek.

"My beautiful daughter, we thought we'd lost you."

"She needs rest," Basil said. "I'll put her on the bed."

Basil strode towards the bedstead, forcing Lord Wilfgive away from his daughter. Isolda had returned from praying in the chapel and was already turning back the bed covers. He gently placed Lynnet on the feather mattress and stepped out of the way. The servant pulled the muddy, bargeman's boots off Lynnet's swollen feet. Evelyn arranged a bolster behind her head and shoulders. Matilda held a goblet of warmed cider to her lips.

"You stink to high heaven!" Lady Durwyn pointed to the Isolda and demanded, "Get our daughter out of those awful clothes and into a bath."

Isolda scurried to the chest for the clean clothing.

"Water is already heating," Evelyn said.

Basil turned to Lynnet's father. He was going to get things settled right away.

"Lord Wilfgive, I've asked your daughter to marry me. She accepted."

"You have my blessing."

Basil's jaw dropped. Her father had given his approval! Basil glanced at Lady Durwyn. Her lips were pressed into a tight, straight line as if to prevent an argument from escaping. He turned back to Lord Wilfgive .

"My waking hours will be to seeing to her happiness."

"A father couldn't ask for more for his daughter."

"I love her."

"When I thought my daughter was dead," Lynnet's father continued, "her happiness is what I offered to God for her safe return. You have my blessing."

Lord Wilfgive gestured towards the bed where Lynnet was undergoing the caring ministrations of Matilda, Evelyn and Isolda.

"Go now. Let the women see to my daughter's comfort. Tomorrow, you and I will discuss the marriage contract and her dowry."

Basil stared, shocked to learn there would be a financial settlement. He'd believed Lynnet would be cut off upon marriage to him.

He bowed to her father.

"My grateful thanks."

He turned and strode towards the still-opened door. It was time to get back to duty. He must find her abductors and make them pay for their crimes.

After getting a bath.

Chapter Twenty-Five

Despite her trepidation as she neared Rosamund's chamber door, Matilda believed she was right that she should be the one to tell her sister-in-law her husband was dead. Matilda understood the emptiness of loss. She was better equipped than her husband to find calming words. Women had been comforting the bereaved for centuries.

When she arrived at the chamber door, she stood there a moment shoring up her courage. When it seemed useless to delay longer, Matilda rapped sharply on the door.

Rosamund looked bewildered as the door swung open.

"Have you come to gloat?"

Matilda winced.

"May I come in? I bring a message from your brother."

"What power do I have to keep you out? As I pack, I expect the soldiers to come and drag me to a cell."

Rosamund threw a forearm up across her forehead.

"How I am betrayed! How could Maximilian do this to me?"

Matilda came farther into the chamber and touched Rosamund's arm.

"I believe you should sit down. I have bad news."

"Bad news?" Rosamund said, pulling away from Matilda's touch. "All I've been getting this past hour is bad news."

Nevertheless, Rosamund sat down. Her maidservant quietly disappeared into a smaller, rear chamber. As Matilda sat down at her sister-in-law's side, she tried to pat her hand, but Rosamund snatched it away.

"Well, what is it?" Rosamund asked sharply.

Matilda would have liked to tell this news more gently, but the woman made it impossible.

"Your husband has been stabbed to death by thieves."

Unexpectedly, Rosamund crumbled before Matilda's eyes. Her face collapsed into a horrified, questioning look. If she had not already been sitting, she would have fallen.

"Maximilian? Not Maximilian."

Matilda reached out and patted her shoulder. Rosamund did not flinch away.

"I'm afraid so."

"How?"

"We don't know details. A courier brought the message. The sheriff's man will be arriving later tonight or tomorrow. Then, we'll know more."

Rosamund shivered uncontrollably. Matilda lifted one of the cloaks set aside for packing and put it around her shoulders.

"Come and lie down. I'll get your maidservant to sit with you."

"Thank you."

Rosamund allowed Matilda to escort her into the bed and tuck her under warm covers. She lay, curled up on her side, her face lost in the bedding.

Matilda hated to leave her with no family near, but Lynnet was her first priority today.

"I'll send someone with warm broth. Your brother will come by later to sit with you."

As Matilda quietly closed the door, the only sound was an anguished keening.

Basil came to her bedchamber that evening after the meal. Evelyn and Isolda discreetly excused themselves and left. He pulled a chair across the room to sit next to the bed. Warmth spread through Lynnet at his closeness. A slight tingling accompanied it. She probably was blushing.

She felt considerably improved now that she had rested and bathed. She was sitting up, the covers pulled to her waist, a warm shawl around her shoulders and her hair pulled under a nightcap. She couldn't be looking her best, but from the warmth in Basil's voice, that didn't matter.

"Your father gave his blessing."

"I heard."

"The two men who abducted you are in Tower cells. The conspirators have confessed. My work for the king is finished."

She reached for his hand, relishing the power it exuded.

"You must be pleased everything ended successfully."

"The deputy has taken charge. I'm to meet with the king at Westminster Palace tomorrow morning. I suspect I'll be relieved of my special commission and ordered back to being Sheriff of London."

Basil wrapped her hand within his and ran a thumb over the back of her knuckles. He had bathed and smelled of soap and freshly washed clothing. His beribboned Seal of Office tickled her wrist as he leaned towards her.

"The king requests your presence at Westminster tomorrow. Do you think you'll be able to travel?"

"I suspect he wants to hear the story of my abduction before he passes judgment. If I can survive a rickety butcher's cart on rutted, winter roads, I can survive a slow ride on a gentle mare to give testimony."

"Speaking of which, your father bought another workhorse and cart for the butcher who drove you to the Tower."

"I'm glad. I know father is offering a dowry as well."

Lynnet could make out against the candlelight that Basil was nodding.

"We're to discuss it tomorrow. It'll have to be after we return from Westminster."

"My mother is furious. It's her family money. She's made father promise that the marriage contract will state the money stays under my control and reverts back to her family if something happens to me. She doesn't want you to benefit."

Basil laughed heartily. "True to form."

"So like my mother."

"That's acceptable to me," Basil said. "The only thing I want from this marriage is you."

"No children?" she asked coquettishly.

"That goes without saying."

"I'd like to wed as soon as possible so you can stay in London," he said. "I fear if you return north with your parents, they'll talk you out of our marriage. At least, your mother would try."

"She'd never succeed."

"Her nagging can be persuasive. Especially against your father."

"He'll respect my wishes. He made a promise to God."

"I worry that tomorrow the king may object to our marriage.

I'm an illegitimate son. You're second cousin to the late queen. King Henry may not think me worthy."

Lynnet stiffened. Such a thought hadn't crossed her mind. With her father still alive, the king didn't have direct control over her. Still, he could withdraw Basil's appointment as sheriff and make life difficult for them.

She clutched at his hand. Tears welled up behind her eyes.

"We cannot be separated again!"

Basil gently removed her hand. For a man of his bulk, he treated her as if fragile and of great value.

Lynnet heard him pull off his boots and allow them to drop with a clunk to the floor. The bed dipped as he crawled in beside her. Her heart pounded in her ears. Hungry lips swept across her temples, alongside her nose and to her waiting mouth.

"I won't let them separate us," he murmured against her lips. "If we must, we'll run away."

She pressed against him, reveling in the heat pouring out of him. An inquisitive hand wandered along her buttocks and lightly tugged her linen nightgown up and out of their way.

She ran the tip of her tongue across his open lips, shivering at the sensations provoked. Basil's breathing increased tenfold as his capable hands roamed her bared skin. She discovered herself moving against him to a primal rhythm previously unknown.

A knock sounded on the door.

"Dammit," Basil muttered, but he was already out of the bed and putting his boots back on.

Lynnet controlled her breathing, pulled her nightgown down and straightened the bedding. Before Basil could turn to answer the door, she grabbed his hand.

"King Henry has known me since I was a child. I'll make him see reason."

He kissed her fingers and went to answer the door.

"Basil," she heard her father say, sounding surprised. "I've come to see to my daughter before she retires."

"Of course, sir. I'll leave you to her. Evelyn will return shortly."

Lynnet's heart speeded up. She hoped there was no leftover sign of Basil in the bedding.

"No, no. As long as you're here, stay. We may as well discuss the marriage contract tonight."

Chapter Twenty-Six

She was fully aware of Basil riding beside her all the time they were traveling to Westminster for their audience with King Henry. Two soldiers rode behind them for protection should friends of André, Courbet or Maximilian plan mischief. So far, it looked as if the three had worked alone with hired underlings.

Stable boys took charge of the horses after Basil helped her down at the palace steps. He ordered the soldiers to wait at the stables and rub down and feed the horses.

With her arm tightly pressed against him, he guided her to the palace entrance. Lynnet was grateful because the early morning light wasn't sufficient for her to differentiate the height and breadth of the stairs.

A page led them to a small chamber. Basil removed his weapons and left them with the guard before entering. He whispered that this chamber was the one where he accepted the king's commission to find the thieves. It would be here that it would be revoked.

Fate is capricious.

Because of the commission, Basil was in the Tower cellars to save her from the conspirators. Because he was a friend of Geoff's, she'd told him what she overheard instead of some other official. She'd wanted to fall in love at winter court so she wouldn't have to obey her parents and accept an arranged marriage and she'd done so.

Such random circumstances coming together to answer my wish.

In the light of many candles, she could make out that the king sat behind a table and his deputy stood nearby. Lynnet was invited to be seated. Basil stood behind her chair, his hand resting on its back, his fingers lightly touching the nape of her neck.

King Henry questioned her about what she overheard and about her two kidnappings. When satisfied, he asked about their betrothal.

"Don't look so surprised, Cousin," the king laughed. "I hear many things. Besides, your father told me of your affection when he came to ask for my help."

Basil answered the king for her. He told how, during the investigation, they had fallen in love.

"And so, Your Majesty, Lady Lynnet agreed to marry me. Her father approves. We seek your blessing on our union."

"You have it."

Basil's knees seemed to be buckling. She heard his clothing slide against the back of her chair. At first, he'd been holding himself rigid while searching for words to win the king over. After the king's blessing, his fingers loosened their grip on her clothing at the nape of her neck.

"I called you here for a different reason," the king was saying. "I command you, Basil of Ipswich, to renew your vow of loyalty to the crown."

Basil stepped out from behind her chair and bowed.

"Honored, Your Majesty."

He knelt, swore allegiance before God and repeated the oath of fidelity after Baron Otheur.

"For faithful duty to the crown," the king said, "you will henceforth be known as Sir Basil of Chester."

Lynnet's heart sang. Basil was being knighted into the king's service.

"You are given charge in my name of your half-brother's forfeited lands in Chester."

Lynnet beamed. Last night's fears were without merit. Along with the generous allowance from her father, she and Basil would have income from two estates. She'd worked herself into a state over nothing, allowing herself to be indiscreet.

It was fortunate our visitor was my father. Evelyn would have walked in without knocking.

"Your father knows of this transfer of property," the king was saying to Basil. "It is an understatement to say he is not pleased to see his legitimate son stripped of his estate."

"He cannot get his teeth around his son's betrayal," Baron Otheur said. "He blames you for Sir André's downfall."

The king nodded his head.

"I want the two of you out of London quickly. I'll keep the earl in town until his temper cools."

"I'll ask Lord Wilfgive to remove Lady Lynnet from London as quickly as possible," Basil replied. "I won't place her in danger again."

Lynnet's spirits plummeted. She'd be dragged away from Basil.

"That's not what I had in mind," King Henry said. "I ask you to be married today by my priest and leave as husband and wife."

"But my parents," Lynnet started to say, her spirits rising.

"They should be on the road to Westminster at this moment," the king said. "My deputy spoke with your father last night. He agreed to a hasty marriage."

Lynnet's heart raced.

"I ordered your clothing packed," the baron said to them. "It should be arriving here shortly."

"The longer you are within reach of the earl, the more likely he'll slip out of my control and start rampaging. I want you on your way early tomorrow. An armed guard will accompany you."

"My companion and servant?"

"Your father told me of your affection for your servants," the deputy said. "They are ordered to Westminster for the wedding ceremony and dinner. Your companion will accompany you to your new home."

Lynnet's head was spinning.

"As well as Lord Geoffrey and Lady Matilda," King Henry added. "They'll be here for your wedding."

"I can't believe they kept this a secret." Basil sounded utterly baffled.

The king rose, indicating the audience was at an end.

"I hope you're not too disappointed, Cousin, with my arrangements. I know young women want to plan their own weddings and their bridal gowns."

Lynnet's heart nearly burst with joy.

"A hasty wedding is exactly what I want," she told her king.

That afternoon, in the Westminster Palace Chapel, Basil waited at the altar. He wore his best, black-wool breeches with knee-length, leather boots. His white linen tunic was topped by a lightweight black cloak hanging to his knees, with slits for his arms.

He was impatiently waiting for the king, his daughter and

his deputy to enter the chapel before Lynnet could appear. Geoff stood at his side as witness. Her parents, Evelyn and Isolda sat on benches. Matilda would accompany the bride as her attendant and a second witness.

When I ran barefoot on the Ipswich wharves, I never dreamed I'd marry a noblewoman, especially an Anglo-Saxon.

He especially never conceived of being married in a palace with the king in attendance. Not until he left the military and became a sheriff did he even entertain the possibility of marriage.

Basil had sent the soldiers who accompanied them from the Tower to his sheriff's quarters in London to pack up his belongings. The rest of his clothing arrived by wagon, along with Lynnet's.

Tonight, we combine those belongings.

His heart beat faster as he imagined being alone with Lynnet with no possibility of her father pounding on the door.

The king and his daughter arrived, resplendent in silks and furs. The dignified deputy followed close behind. They sat in the only pew, one of hand-carved oak, high-backed, with a red velvet cushion, and a kneeling rail. The small chapel, designed for only the king's family, felt crowded.

Basil turned back to the altar where the priest was chanting as he lighted tapered white candles in tall, gold candlesticks. The altar was covered by a white lace cloth. An altar boy swung a bronze, open-faced ball from a chain. Incense permeated the chapel.

A stirring alerted Basil that his bride had arrived. His breath caught in his throat when he turned to watch Lynnet walk to him.

She's exquisite.

Matilda had chosen a light blue, linen gown which hugged Lynnet's slender figure and trailed behind her as she walked. A large, intricate golden brooch on her right shoulder held the garment closed.

Tonight, that spiked brooch will be the first to go.

A golden girdle circled her waist, denying him access.

That girdle will be the second to go.

A white, shoulder-length veil concealed her expression.

She carried a small, white leather prayer book, one that normally rested on the chapel lectern. Although Lynnet didn't embrace the new religion, she agreed, at the king's suggestion, to a Catholic ceremony to appease the Earl of Chester.

Matilda walked at Lynnet's left side. As they passed the benches, Lord Wilfgive rose and accompanied them to the altar. Lynnet handed the prayer book to Matilda. She searched for Basil's hand before facing the priest, who was already chanting. His body warmed to her touch, despite the chill of the unheated chapel.

We'll soon be one.

Basil didn't know if Lynnet understood Latin. She was educated, but he didn't know how far. Being nobility, she may have been taught the language.

With everything happening these past two weeks, the only thing he really knew about this woman was that his body yearned incessantly for her and his immortal soul would embrace her lovingly for all time.

She is my joy.

The priest intoned the soothing Latin words Basil memorized as a student of the monks. The monastery training would serve him well as he administered his new estate. No bailiff could cheat him nor a clerk be able to falsify the records.

Her father gave away the bride and returned to Lady Durwyn, who looked less opposed to the marriage than she did yesterday.

It's best Lynnet not be estranged from her family, although I'll not agree to visit often.

The speed of everything happening had numbed him. The straw he clutched to keep his equilibrium was the woman standing serenely at his side. In marriage, she'd soothe him after his struggles in an oft times vicious world. She possessed the charm to quiet his restless soul.

The priest asked for the ring.

Basil froze, shocked. He'd forgotten about this symbol of faithfulness. He could only stutter in Latin, "I...I have none."

Lord Otheur rose. Reaching into his pocket, he brought out a golden wedding band.

"My regrets, Father. I should have remembered this sooner. The king presents this ring as his gift to his cousin."

Gratefully, Basil accepted. Later, he'd buy Lynnet her own ring.

For now, a band carved with flowers will do.

Basil slipped the ring on Lynnet's finger, pledging his love. Repeating after the priest, his bride swore her troth, after which the priest pronounced them married.

He lifted the filmy, white veil covering Lynnet's face and draped it behind her. Her face glowed with love.

I discovered this jewel under a broken crate in a musty cellar.

Basil cupped her face and slowly bent towards her. Lynnet's scent drew him like a flower draws a bee. He brushed her lips, tasting the soft, salty flesh and then settled more solidly against them. The tip of her tongue slowly touched his bottom lip, causing his manhood to rise.

Releasing her face, Basil pulled Lynnet passionately into his arms. Bending her backwards, he deepened their kiss. An irritated "hrrummphh" from Lady Durwyn forced him to remember their audience.

Basil released her and looked at his bride. Lynnet smiled, privately, secretively, as if she knew what lay ahead.

Could any wish be more happily fulfilled? I am wed at winter court to a man I adore.

Laughter and excited voices filled the small chamber off the chapel where a meal had been arranged by Lynnet's parents. A huge fire roared in the fireplace. Multi-branched candelabra cast dancing figures on the walls.

Lady Durwyn had spent the few hours at Westminster before the wedding ceremony haranguing the chamberlain and kitchen help to see that the finest linens and utensils decked the wedding table. She had chosen the finest of the foods prepared for the evening meal. She had had a servant at the ready outside the chapel to run to the kitchens to alert them to bring the food hot and quickly. Golden goblets were set out for a toast to the bride and groom. Wine and food overflowed and more lay in reserve on a wheeled cart.

Basil had cut up her food for her, but the butterflies in her stomach kept her from swallowing.

Geoff sat next to Basil, the two men swapping stories. Matilda sat next to her and her parents and Evelyn across the table. Isolda chose to help serve.

The king and his deputy had business elsewhere, but his daughter joined the wedding celebration. Lynnet's mother possessively assigned Lady Maude to sit next to her.

Lynnet overheard her mother whispering loudly to Evelyn.

"Well, I can't do anything about his being Norman, but at least he has an estate and money."

Lynnet chuckled. She'd gotten the best of the bargain.

Because of Basil, she'd never again cower in darkened fear, hiding from her mother's sharp tongue. His strength gave her courage.

She'd noticed, since Basil proposed, she no longer dwelt on her disability. He made it of such little consequence, she felt a whole woman.

She didn't know what challenges children would bring, but with the money they would receive, Lynnet knew she could keep their children safe.

Thinking about what they must do to make children brought on a hot flush. Basil's wedding kiss provided an intriguing taste. She longed for this feast to end and her friends and family to leave. She yearned to be alone with this man she loved fiercely.

Lynnet felt a presence and looked up. Her grandmother hovered in a darkened corner. She seemed to be nodding her head.

I'm glad you approve, Grandmamma. Just don't follow us to our bedchamber.

Basil impatiently paced the corridor outside their wedding bedchamber, waiting for Matilda to finish preparing Lynnet for bed. Geoff tried to convince him to stay at the banquet table until Matilda returned there, but Basil shook off commonsense. No minute must be wasted now that he had society's approval to bed Lynnet.

Anticipation and apprehension warred.

What if Lynnet believed she'd made a mistake when faced with the physical side of marriage? It had been only a few weeks that they'd known each other. They had only scratched the surface of understanding. He didn't know what rejection by her would do to him.

He stopped pacing, realizing that all his life, when faced by problems, he plunged right in to resolve them. He could be no different with Lynnet. She must love him for himself, whatever his virtues or faults.

The door opened abruptly. He looked up to see Matilda's startled face.

"Basil. You're here already."

"How's Lynnet?"

"She's fine." Matilda moved away from the door. "She's waiting for you."

As Matilda hurried away down the corridor, Basil entered the chamber and softly shut the door. Lynnet lay propped up on pillows against the dark wood headboard of a four-poster draped with heavy, green velvet. The several layers of covers were tucked in around her waist. Her silky, flaxen hair flowed across the pillows. Matilda must have brushed it until it glowed in the candlelight. Her white-linen, sleeved nightgown fastened at the neck by a long-stringed ribbon. Lynnet held her arms out to him.

"Husband."

Basil wrenched his cloak over his head and flung it to the floor. Already striding towards his beloved, he stripped off the linen tunic and threw it down. His bared chest felt the chamber's chill despite a blazing fire in the fireplace. One candle burned on a nightstand next to the bed.

Hopping on one foot, Basil yanked off his knee-length, leather boot and dropped it to the stone floor. The other soon followed suit. He started untying the knot at his trouser waistband, and stopped.

I'd best wait.

He pulled off his socks instead.

By that time, his hopping had taken him to the bed. Lynnet had heard him coming and she changed the angle of her arms.

Basil lifted the bedcovers, gazing in the light from the candle and the fireplace at the slender form of his beautiful wife.

I am so blessed.

He deftly laid himself between her outstretched arms.

Seeking her waiting mouth, Basil kissed his way up her throat, over her chin and to her lips. His throat dry, his chest constricted, he explored the sensations aroused as her hands studied his body.

Plunging his hands into her fine, fair hair, he raised her head slightly so that his tongue could probe the hot, moist depths of her mouth. Her tongue challenged his as his breath arrived in short gasps. His heart pounded as if trying to break through his chest. His mind spun wildly.

As Lynnet's hands explored his bared back, Basil's breathing became more ragged. She investigated muscle by muscle, probing and moving on. His skin heated to boiling. He was glad he hadn't pulled up the covers when he'd entered the bed.

Propping himself on elbows to keep from crushing his bride, Basil dexterously stretched out his legs on either side of her, knees bent to hold his weight. Even slightly raised above her, Lynnet must know how ready he was.

Basil turned his head enough to find the bottom of her nightgown. He grabbed hold of the hem. The side of his hand grazed Lynnet's warmed skin as he drew the cloth upward, precariously keeping his body weight lifted. When the cloth caught on her bottom, Lynnet raised her hips against him and worked the cloth up towards her neck. Basil's heated flesh touched her softness from her womanhood to her bosom.

Good God in heaven!

Relaxing downward on his elbows, hoping he was not crushing her, he used both hands to untie her nightgown and pull it off her arms and over her head. He held it out over the edge of the bed and dropped it to the floor, feeling a sense of triumph.

Urgently needing her, Basil reached for her breast, squeezed and sighed. The raised nipple declared her desire for him.

I need not have worried.

His attention was drawn to her hands untying the knot at his waistband. His breath caught in his throat. Her knuckles pressed into his belly as she worked the knots, causing ripples of desire. She kissed him when she succeeded, then inched the cloth down over his buttocks, exercising every opportunity to stroke his skin.

Her body moved rhythmically, causing a torment that jangled his nerves. Sweat raised a light sheen of moisture on his skin. She reached between his legs to release the trouser cloth caught on his manhood. He shuddered when she ran her fingertips along the shaft.

Merciful heavens.

She stroked him and guided him towards her, helping him adjust to their differing sizes. He raised his hips to allow Lynnet to wrap her legs around his back. She guided him until he touched her moist womanhood, then sighed and dropped back onto the feather mattress. He probed before pushing inside.

Mysterious, intriguing, it was as if he touched a sacred portal. Unguarded, he believed, when opened, it would rival the treasures of the world.

He could contain himself no longer. He pushed past her virginity and felt her close around him. Unsatisfied, he pushed towards her innermost secrets.

Her body sweated. She cried out and gasped for air.

Basil worried he had hurt her until she clutched him tighter to herself. Basil matched Lynnet's rhythm, marveling at the sensations.

Raised to fever pitch, she screamed, "Husband," as her body spasmed. Matching her frenzy, Basil spilled his seed in pumping gushes then rolled, quivering, onto his side, taking her with him, still locked together in satiated love.

"I have no words to express the love I feel for you," Basil said, nuzzling her ear.

"I never expected to know such love."

Feeling the chilled air on his cooling skin, he pulled the covers up around her, regretting all the while that he could no longer see her beautiful body.

He reached over, unhooked the bed drapery where it was anchored to the bedpost, letting the heavy folds hang. A cocoon of pure blackness descended, making him Lynnet's equal. He reached out, touching this sightless woman. Somehow, she brought him out of the darkness of loneliness and into the light of her love.

He stroked the length of her body.

"We need to leave at first light," he said, trying to be practical. "A delay would annoy the king and have possible repercussions with my father."

"We can't have that," she agreed.

He kissed her forehead lightly.

"I want to make love again, but if we stay awake too late, we'll be tired tomorrow."

"It would be difficult traveling when exhausted," she agreed.

"We have much to learn about each other. We only touched the surface of where love can take us."

He caressed her nipple, while she probed between his legs.

"I'm eager to learn."

"Tomorrow, we travel side by side to our new home."

"It's a journey to occupy us the rest of our lives."

"If we're wise, we would get our rest."

"You're probably right, Husband," she said as she stroked him.

They were silent for a while as their breathing came under control and their bodies cooled from their lovemaking.

He grinned and whispered in her ear, "Let's throw wisdom out the window. I'd like to see what else we can teach each other about love."

"With that I definitely agree," she said as she shifted closer.

About the Author

When JoAnn Smith Ainsworth carried wood so her Great Aunt Martha could stoke up the iron stove to prepare dinner, the pre-teen wasn't thinking, "I could use this in a novel someday." Yet almost 60 years later, the skills she learned from her horse-and-buggy ancestors translate into a backdrop for her historical romance novels.

JoAnn is a graduate of the University of California, Berkeley, with a double major in English and Social Science. She has her Masters in Teaching English from Fairleigh Dickinson University and her M.B.A. studies from Pepperdine University.

She likes to walk, swim and read.

To learn more, please visit www.joannsmithainsworth.com.

Haunted by war, a thief finds salvation in the arms of an angel.

Devils on Horseback: Jake

© 2008 Beth Williamson

Devils on Horseback, Book Two

On the surface, Jake Sheridan is an easygoing man whose problems roll off him like water off a duck's back. Truth is, Jake holds so many past demons inside him, he daren't let them out for fear he'll never get them all back in.

He and the Devils are hired to help rebuild a town ransacked by marauders. Everywhere they turn, they encounter secrets—enough secrets to turn the town to dust if they don't uncover the truth.

Only one person in town isn't glad to see them: Gabrielle Rinaldi, the miller's daughter. A strong and independent woman who is used to being disrespected for speaking her mind, she makes no secret that she doesn't believe hired guns are the answer to the town's woes. Yet she finds herself drawn to the enigmatic and charming Jake.

In spite of himself, Jake falls hard and fast for Gabby. But she's wary of handing her heart to a man who lives by his guns.

When tragedy strikes, Jake and Gabby must fight to find a way to save the town—and their hearts.

Warning, this title contains the following: explicit sex, graphic language, violence.

There's more to this man than satin and lace.

Met by Chance

© 2008 Lynne Connolly

Book 3 of the Triple Countess series

After a serious riding accident, Perdita Garland is back in society. Unfortunately the first man who catches her interest, Charles Dalton, Marquis of Petherbridge, turns out to be a popinjay with a spoiled daughter in tow. And his equally spoiled sister is flirting with the same fortune-hunting suitor who almost cost Perdita her life. What's a lady to do? Warn the marquis of the danger, of course.

Charles knows that English society finds his manners and dress astonishing, but they cover a man broken by a disastrous marriage to a faithless wife. Now a widowed father determined not to be fooled again, he is nevertheless charmed by Perdita and the steely strength of will under her fragile exterior. If only the lady would mind her own business.

But when his impulsive sister elopes and kidnaps his daughter, he finds himself wishing he had listened to the little busybody. And Perdita, feeling partly responsible for the disaster, boldly sets out to help him put things right.

Alone in a strange city with his lordship, plunged into danger, Perdita discovers there is more than meets the eye under the pampered skin of the marquis. There is strength, power...and passion beyond her wildest dreams.

Printed in the United States
145180LV00001B/45/P

9 781605 042770